MAKING IT RAIN IN TEXAS

An Al Quinn Novel

RUSS HALL

Making It Rain in Texas
An Al Quinn© Novel
Red Adept Publishing, LLC
104 Bugenfield Court
Garner, NC 27529
http://RedAdeptPublishing.com/

Chapter One

"How'd you get along all those years as a sheriff's department detective when you're such an introvert?"

Al turned onto his side to look right at Fergie. She pulled the sheet up to her bare shoulders. He had been thinking about getting up for the last half hour as the room grew brighter while the sun rose. Her skin was surprisingly smooth. Her long red hair spread out across her pillow. A tiny shadow line of grey was peeking through at the roots of her part, but that was easy enough to shrug off.

"I'm not an introvert. Here I am in bed with a beautiful woman. To wit: you. I have a dog as well as a brother, his much younger bride, and a baby in my house. It's a regular Grand Central Station around here."

"Not by your choice, and having a dog isn't in your favor on the introvert ticket. Most of the rest was against your will. You'd planned to live alone. You like to fish alone. And you used to take hikes by yourself, go to the gym by yourself, as well as grocery shop and cook for yourself."

He cupped one hand to the side of his face as he lifted himself up onto his elbow. "You're leaving out the part about 'desirable you' being in my bed."

"Look. I'm in my sixties, same as you. Won't be too long before I'm sporting a walker and am tottering around here, trying to remember why I left one room for another."

"But you'll still have your looks. You have to give me that."

He shifted to lie on his back. She moved closer. Outside the closed blinds of the bedroom window, a cardinal went on and on in his mating call for a spell. Al halfway listened to it. Then a mockingbird took over with a more inventive call. Some folks, he knew, considered the mockingbird a pest, didn't like its strident tunes. But at least it was less repetitive than that cardinal. The mockingbird ate bugs too, tons of them: grasshoppers, crickets, and even mosquitoes. He'd even seen a mockingbird catch a flying cicada in midair and gulp it down, a feat in proportion to Al swallowing a football.

"What are you thinking about?" Fergie nuzzled closer.

"Just enjoying our quiet time together."

Off in another room, in the basement, the baby began to cry. Little Al. Al's nephew, now a part of his household.

"I was just savoring the notion that we have nothing on our plates for a spell and could delight in staying late in bed as long as we want," Al said.

Someone banged on Al's bedroom door.

"Who is it?" Fergie called out.

"You gotta come out! We've got a problem!" Bonnie yelled through the door. "A really serious problem."

"If it's the baby, I don't change diapers," Al said.

"Not to worry. Maury's on that case, much against his will."

"Figures. I was enjoying sleeping in and really feeling retired for a change," Al said.

He climbed out of bed, ignoring the wolf whistle Fergie gave him.

"What is it? What's wrong?" he called out while tugging on his jeans.

"We've been robbed!"

"When you say 'we,' Bonnie, just who do you mean?"

"The hospital, at least our charity group, has been robbed."

Al had seen the few donation jars in the hospital's gift shop and had gotten a donation form in the mail. Outside the hospital, a thermometer-shaped billboard measured the charity's progress toward its goal.

He buttoned up his shirt but kept an eye on Fergie.

"Go on and get out there." Fergie pulled the sheet closer. "I don't want you becoming the lecher your brother used to be."

"Really?"

He shook his head. She had just spent the night naked in bed beside him and more than a little sweaty for part of that, and now this. He shared an exaggerated sigh and took his boots and socks and went out the door, closing it behind him.

Bonnie was waiting, standing far too close.

Al held up a forefinger. "Coffee first."

She scampered off to get him a mug. He sat at one of the dining-table chairs and tugged on his socks and boots. Through the row of windows lining the wall, he could look out across Lake Travis. A light breeze was casting a set of silver ripples on the surface. Even though the lake level was dropping, today would have been a darn good day to take the boat out onto the lake and catch a few fish. Only recently, Fergie had started to tag along and do some fishing as well. At first, he thought he would miss his time alone on the water. But he was enjoying her company even when now and again she caught more or bigger fish.

He sat waiting until Bonnie brought a steaming mug and slipped it in front of him with enough vigor for a little to slop out over one side.

"Now what is it that has you in such a doo dah?" he asked.

She started to sit down at the table then stood back up, too twitchy to settle. Bonnie was still about the same size she'd been before having the baby, and she had what Maury called the build of a muffin. She was also a youthful thirty-seven, while Maury, Fergie, and Al were all in their sixties. The age issue was relative but made her seem a frustrated teen when she was agitated, as she was at the moment.

"Now slowly," he said, "tell me. Is it the hospital itself, or that little charity effort in which you've been involved?"

"It isn't little," she snapped. "Not by a long shot!"

"How much are we talking about?"

"Two hundred and seventy thousand dollars."

Al had his mug halfway to his mouth and lowered it.

"Come again?"

"You heard me." She raised a hand to move a strand of curly blond hair back away from her brow. Her hand quivered. "We were almost to our goal of three hundred thousand."

"And you're responsible?"

"You've met our boss, Hermina Vanderhausen, the administrator at the hospital. I'm sure you think that it's with nothing but affection that they call her The Hammer and that she's all goodness and light around the place, since she gave Maury and me both jobs at a time when we needed them."

"I didn't know what to think of her," Al said. "We met only briefly, and she looked a bit like the late Queen Victoria might if she wore spurs."

"Well, she's all spurs right now. And I'm the one she's digging them into."

"You'd better explain," Al said.

"This was for cancer, and the hospital okayed getting an experienced fund-raiser. And, yes, it was my idea. I was team captain of the ones rounding up donations for our hospital."

The baby began to cry again. Its crib was downstairs on the floor Maury and Bonnie shared since they'd gotten married.

"Just a minute." She took off and scampered down the stairs.

Fergie came out of the bedroom and gave Al one of her patented raised-eyebrow looks while she went across to pour herself a mug of coffee from the thermos by the sink. At a lanky six feet two, she looked quite a contrast to bouncy Bonnie, who Al doubted stood much above five feet tall.

"I thought Little Al was in day care at the hospital," Al said.

Fergie eased into one of the dining chairs beside him and lowered the mug she had just raised to her mouth. "When they gave Bonnie back her job as a nurse, they had her in the oncology ward. But they had to move her out of there, and she's doing a night shift until they can find her a new day spot in some other ward. Maury's still on days as the safety inspector. But today's his day off."

"I never thought I'd hear the words 'safety inspector' in the same breath as his name." Al shook his head. He took a sip of coffee. "Why did Bonnie get moved from a ward? I thought she was fairly passionate about that sort of thing, since her mother died from cervical cancer not long after lung cancer took out her father."

"She's passionate, all right. Too much so. She started coming in and visiting the patients in her off hours, got far too attached to them. And when they lost one, as they too often do in that ward, she was a mess. Vanderhausen got wind of what Bonnie was doing and decided it had to stop for Bonnie's own good. Say what you will about being a tough boss, she has a heart."

"Who has a heart?" Bonnie emerged from the stairway from downstairs and crossed the living room toward them.

"Your boss, the one who hired you and Maury," Al said.

"You wouldn't think so now if you'd heard her chewing us out for losing this kind of money."

"Really?"

"Really," Bonnie said. "We could lose our jobs, which we need very much right now."

"Are you sure you're not overreacting?" Fergie asked.

Bonnie shook her head hard enough to toss her blond curls about. "You have to understand what kind of woman she is. We had a new head of medical records who thought he was trying to do the hospital a favor by raking in more money. He implemented medical codings that patients couldn't figure out in their billing. It was a way of overpricing everyday things. You know, where a 'thermal therapy kit' is an ice pack, and a 'mucous recovery system' is a box of tissues. An aspirin costs twenty dollars, and a toothbrush can cost in the hundreds. A lot of hospitals were doing it as a way to pad the bills. But Vanderhausen said, 'Not us,' and that guy was out on his ear."

"Why are you in trouble?" Fergie asked.

"Because I'm the one who wanted us to do a cancer fund-raiser. I pushed and pushed until the hospital took it on."

"Back to this theft," Al said. "Who was responsible for that much money when it disappeared?"

"The fund-raiser we hired. A regular pro from Dover at that sort of thing, if her resumé is to be believed. Cynthia Standerblum. She's what they call a rainmaker. Politicians use them a lot when they want to raise money. And we were between elections and their campaigns. She came highly recommended."

"Have you all talked with her about where the money might have gone?"

"We'd sure like to, but she's as gone as the dodo. She had a one-room apartment, and it's as empty as a place can get. And The Hammer is both embarrassed and enraged. And you don't want to see her riled up."

"Who did the background check on her?" Al asked.

"HR, and they said everything checked out. But when they called back to some of the numbers they'd checked, some of them didn't even work anymore."

"Sounds like this wasn't just a casual accident," Al said.

"And for that kind of money, this sounds like a pro all right, but the wrong kind." Fergie started to lift her mug, realized it was empty, and put it back down. "I suppose you checked with the city police department, but they've had their own problems. Someone was just recently using the police-department number for an IRS scam that intimidated some people into giving up their credit-card numbers over the phone."

"Did they catch who was doing that?" Bonnie asked.

"Of course not," Fergie said. "That sort of outfit is very slick. Not to mention daring. Imagine using the police department's phone number to scam people."

"Do you think our Cynthia Standerblum is that slick? She's certainly that daring, to brazenly gain our trust and work with us until we were almost to our goal. We would have all been so proud to be doing good and fighting cancer as best we know how."

"I'll make you one bet right now," Al said.

"What's that?" Bonnie asked.

"That her real name isn't Cynthia Standerblum."

"What does Hermina Vanderhausen plan to do about it?" Fergie asked. "I imagine she's already filed a police report. But it's not the sort of thing their vice squad handles."

"Don't I know. We were referred to the Office of the Attorney General of Texas. They handle frauds and scams. But I sense that the complaint form we completed for them is stacked in a pile of others waiting for attention."

"And?" Fergie said.

"Well." Bonnie looked down then slowly lifted her head. "Vanderhausen is going to fire me for sure and Maury too. We were kind of hoping you two could do something. I told her I'd ask you two to help. She was okay with that... if you can fix this. You know, being as how you're both retired detectives. It was the first and only hope she had of getting that money back."

"I hope you stressed the word 'retired' when you spoke with her," Al said.

"I mentioned it, but she rolled right over me. She was sure you were the sort of people who couldn't resist doing a good deed if you had the chance."

"That makes us seem more like suckers than champions," Al said.

"Tomato, potato. You'll do it, won't you? Please! I meant it about her being ready to fire us like two shots out of a cannon."

AL PATTED TANNER ON the head and closed the front door before Tanner could rush outside and follow them. Al saw the dog's tail stop wagging, which bothered him. A whole lot of things got to him these days in ways they never had before. *Getting old.* He and Fergie went across to his truck. He was just climbing into his side when his cell phone rang.

He answered it as he slid inside. "Well, if it isn't Sheriff Clayton. To what do I owe—"

"This is no honor," Clayton snapped. "I need to ask a favor. Every detective I've got is up to his earlobes in half a dozen cases."

"You do recall I'm retired, don't you?"

"You're probably just sitting around on your hands wishing you had something to do, right?"

"Not really."

"Listen up. This is easy. Can you do it?"

"Better tell me what it is first."

"You'd never get away with that attitude if you were back in the department."

"Hello? Retired?"

"Okay. Okay. I really need your help on this, so I'll put up with your whatever. Call it sass."

"Go ahead."

"There's been a chupacabra spotting."

"For heaven's sake."

"It's over kind of in your neck of the woods, or I wouldn't ask."

"What happened to your animal-control people?"

"This isn't really about an animal, Al. You know that. It's about the people who believe in it and think they've spotted one. They're your kind of people."

"Me and Jerry Springer, right?"

"You know what I mean. I'm just asking the favor."

Al didn't mention that almost every postretirement favor Clayton had asked of him had damn near gotten Al killed, and Fergie along with him, more than once. But he couldn't see where this one would do any harm. Of course, he could be wrong.

"Okay. Where is this chupacabra?"

"All the way northwest, almost on the Burnet County border. I'll have Dahlia, my new aide, text you the coordinates."

Al closed the connection and put away his phone.

"Oh, boy. We hardly ever got chupacabra calls in the city," Fergie said. "Except on full moons and Halloween. I'd kind of like to see one. Sort of a hairless coyote that sucks blood from goats and livestock, right?"

"That's the four-one-one on that. I don't believe they exist."

"Then why the call?"

"Clayton probably just wants to calm some folks down before they go 'bongo in the Congo' over this, the way some people can do. If it wasn't so damned hot here, they'd be seeing yetis."

"So you're going to look into this?"

"After we mess about with Bonnie's problem. We don't want her and Maury to lose their jobs just when they started to get self-sufficient."

"And stopped sponging off you, right?"

"Tomato, potato," Al said. "We've just got a crook we need to find. We've both managed to do that before."

Chapter Two

Al pulled the truck into the parking lot of a place called Madrigal Joe's Coffee Shop, where he and Fergie had spent some time on a stakeout once. The rainbow flag rising gently in the hot breeze out front didn't affect either of them. The coffee was darn good, and the place had free Wi-Fi. Besides, the clientele were mostly neighborhood sorts. The fact that some patrons were guys who liked guys or girls who liked girls didn't bother Al. At his age, he felt pretty bulletproof to all that, and if some guy were to hit on him, it would just be a good chuckle, especially with Fergie sitting at the same table.

He got his laptop case out of the extended cab. They headed across the gravel to the side door, the warm air lifting Fergie's long red hair out behind her.

She had the computer booted up and ready by the time he brought two oversized mugs to their table. "I got us both the bottomless cup special. I expect we'll soon be riding a righteous caffeine buzz."

"What are we looking for, Al? I figure the hospital's human resources had pretty much exhausted all possibilities on this gal."

"What we have to count on," Al said, "is that she didn't just disappear. She has probably just shifted into another persona, and we can almost depend on the next scam being different but potentially lucrative."

He took a sip of coffee. "I'm going to be up front with you. We've both solved murders, and some pretty tangled and difficult ones. But what we're looking into here is quicksand."

"I agree."

"Have you ever tackled anything like this?" he asked.

"I had a few murder cases and even a robbery or two that would have made excellent crime-show fodder. On the face of them, they seemed impossible to solve. Yet without a tip, a snitch, or the help of some gifted psychic, I somehow got to the other end, and with enough for the DA's people to do their thing."

"I thought as much. I had a few of those as well. But even I'm the first to admit that the world of first-class swindlers and cons is one of smoke and mirrors, followed by another little puff of smoke, and then they're gone."

"I was always glad I didn't have to work frauds," she said. "They may seem white collar, but these are the criminals most like hit men. They don't work out of a moment of passion and leave messy traces all over the place. They have a calculated plan and an exit route in mind, and they have almost no emotion invested in the act. I've seen snakes with warmer hearts. But the worst is that no one, and I mean no one, is better at wiping out a trail, since they started on that process before they began the fraud."

"You'll get no argument from me on that. All we can hope for are the barest threads of connection or involvement to crimes with a similar skill set, crimes that may have already happened or soon will."

"How do I begin to find something as vague as that?"

"Just browse around until you smell something that seems just a little shady enough to be an opportunity for someone like Cynthia, or whatever her name is by now. We'll follow the scent of that if we just get a whiff."

Fergie had been at it for a cup and a half of coffee and hadn't found any trace of her, but she had located a dozen or so fraud prospects or possibilities that might interest Cynthia. She looked up from her computer screen. "Oh, my lord."

Al glanced toward the coffee shop's front door, where she was staring. A wide fellow with black stubbled cheeks around a thick mustache was waddling inside. He grinned, and his teeth shone like a string of overly white pearls.

She turned to Al. "You called him, didn't you?"

"Had to. Everyone else is apparently swinging and missing so far. This Cynthia, or whatever her name really is, is good. I'm suspecting she runs the bamboozle for a living while padding away a pretty good retirement fund at the same time."

Fergie frowned. "Meat Jenkins. Are you sure your calling instead of visiting him at his place wasn't just to avoid his unique blend of halitosis and BO?"

"Those are aspects of his personality that go along with his being the sheriff's department's particular resident techno genius, but no. Not all IT wizards possess his aromatic skills, though he can surefire knock you back a few steps with his presence. But he can dig as deep as anyone on the internet, and if that's her real name, she is plain off the grid."

Meat held up a finger and went over to the counter to place an order. In a few minutes, he came toward their little table. Fergie seemed to be bracing herself.

Al pointed up. "Ceiling fans are going, the AC is at full blast, and we're in a neutral setting where we can make a getaway if need be. Just remember—for the moment, we need him."

The more Al thought about Meat's looks and personality in general, and aroma, he seemed just one more unique individual on the planet, pretty much like all the other examples in the coffee shop. Putting aside his personal habits and hygiene, he was likeable and trustworthy, although his loyalty to Clayton was greater than that to Al. He was himself and had his own unique sense of identity. Even when talking to himself in third person, he referred to himself as "Meat," so he was comfortable in how others saw him. *Well, good for him.*

Meat slid his tray onto the table. A tiny white cup of espresso was dwarfed by a couple of bear claws and three walnut-and-cranberry scones, thinly disguised giant cookies that weren't fooling anyone.

"Howdy," he said to Fergie. "Al." He reached for one of the scones and took a giant bite. Crumbs clung to his mustache like survivors clinging to the side of the *Titanic*.

"Still on a diet, I see," Al said.

"I'm thinking of putting the notion of a diet on a perpetual state of 'maybe tomorrow.' I fought the good fight, but it's bigger than me."

Fergie started to say something and stopped herself.

"I'll cut to the chase," Meat said, lifting his tiny cup to his mouth for a sip. "There is no chase. This woman you asked about is just plain long gone."

"Really? Even *you* couldn't find anything on the great wide universe of the internet?" Al said.

Meat nodded toward their computer. "How have you done in your poking so far?"

"Not good," Fergie admitted. "Not good at all."

"And you won't. Not by that name, at least. Oh, there were tiny scraps here and there, but they're not even bread crumbs." He reached for one of the bear claws on his plate.

Al thought of a thing or two he could say about crumbs but felt remarkable control and managed to say nothing. He stared at some bits of food sprinkled across Meat's mustache and others appearing between those especially bright teeth.

"What would you do if you were us?" Fergie asked.

"I'm guessing you'll have to gumshoe it a bit in the traditional way, maybe start at the hospital. Do you know anyone there?"

"One or two," Fergie said.

She packed up their laptop and stood.

"I'd like to wish you luck." Meat stayed seated. "But I personally doubt very much you'll find a thing if I couldn't find a single digital footprint."

AL AND FERGIE WALKED across an asphalt parking lot. The late-morning heat that smelled of tar rose from its surface. This was going to be another scorcher of a day, and the thermometer had taken off in a gallop upward at dawn and was still climbing. The hospital towered behind them with its full HR department. But no one in it had been able to track down Cynthia Standerblum even though her references had all cleared during the earlier background check. Fergie carried the file containing little more than what was turning out to be a quite good but mostly bogus resume and one semi-blurry photo of the so-called rainmaker beside a patient. Bonnie had said the woman usually avoided getting her picture taken, which Bonnie had supposed came from good-hearted altruism. Al thought otherwise.

"I expected as much," Fergie said. "I don't know when I've seen less of a trail to follow. That woman was good."

"And the ones who checked her references were either exceptionally lax, or this woman has a system behind her designed for just this sort of thing. Build up an identity that seems ironclad but can as quickly be folded up, and off she goes to some new identity and fresh scam."

Al unlocked his truck's doors and climbed in to start it. He cranked the AC up to an icicles-on-eyebrows level. He waved Fergie inside as soon as the heated air in the cab was all gone.

She reached to the dash to turn the blower down. "Unless you plan to hang a side of beef in here."

He nodded. "Just a little overcompensation." He pulled out of the parking lot into the flow of Austin traffic. "I worry when our techie friend Meat Jenkins says there is no traceable Cynthia Standerblum in

Texas or the rest of America for all he can find. And you know he didn't just depend on your regular search engines. He used every bit of resources at his disposal, and you know that is considerable."

"I've never felt so helpless before." Fergie shook her head and looked out her side window.

"I think that's the objective of a good scammer," Al said. "They fill you with confidence and trust early on and leave you howling at the moon later."

"She accomplished that," Fergie said. "What can we do?"

"We're doing it."

He drove out into what should have been thick, green rolling hills of Texas hill country, a view that usually comforted him since it was so like that around his own house. This year, everything was brown or pale yellow. The drought so far had been accompanied by an unbroken string of one-hundred-degree days. The forecasts offered no hope soon. As for the hills, folks from elsewhere who think Texas is as flat as a fritter get quite a jolt when they drive through the ups and downs of twisting roads with all the usually verdant growth, away from the cattle and goat pastures or fields of oil wells or cotton.

During the drought a few years back, Al had provided food daily for a starving herd of deer that grew to thirty then forty. Hunters who brought in deer from the wilds said their stomachs were filled with juniper because nothing else was available to eat. Al had seen hummingbirds swoop down and drink from the stream of water coming from the end of his hose as he watered his bushes and plants to keep them alive. Squirrels came down and dug holes in the wet ground of his potted plants to hunker down against the heat, and they took off up into trees with small succulent plants, since they had no water to drink. This year, the hills and dips into small valleys and arroyos weren't green at all, and Al had already visited the feed store to stock up on food for the deer that would soon be crowding in greater numbers around his house.

All too soon, Al pulled his truck into a church parking lot.

"Why...?" Fergie caught herself when she saw the name of the church on its entrance sign. "Oh, this was one of her references on her resume, and it apparently really exists. I guess I expected to find just an empty lot at the address."

"It's one of only two references that turned out to exist," Al said. "But that raises some questions as well."

The sign proclaimed Church of the Cedar Woods. The building was small, white, and made of wood and had a classic white steeple. The parking lot was just big enough to handle a small congregation of two or three hundred. Al had heard of Texas churches with far more massive followings, like Lakewood Church in Houston, which averaged about fifty-two thousand attendees a week. The Second Baptist Church, also in Houston, had an attendance of about half that. This cute little church in the country, with its paint beginning to chip, could be dropped into and lost in any one of those.

Since Al wished to have words with the pastor, Paul Randall Sinders, he headed for the small house beside the church, which he judged to be the parsonage.

The woman who answered the doorbell wiped her hands on her red-checked apron. A smudge of flour on one cheek and more in her greying hair hinted she'd been baking.

"Oh, you'll find him in his office yonder." She nodded toward the church. "He'll be in his office, whipping up a sermon that ought to rattle the sinners to the bottoms of their socks."

Al could see only one other car parked in the church lot.

As they walked across to the church, Fergie said, "That's the thing about having worked my whole career as a city detective. I missed out on the folksy charm of how folks talk out here."

"I don't know that you've missed a lot. I've met some of them who just prattle on and on, delighted at the way their own voice sounds."

At the church door, Al hesitated, wondering if he should knock. But that wasn't the way of country churches. He reached for the handle and found the door unlocked. He swung it open, and they went inside.

The foyer opened into a small interior, too small for an apse or anything fancy. But Al quite liked the oak woodwork of the trim, lit by rays of colored light coming in through stained-glass windows. Two sides of rows of pews were divided by a center aisle, perfect for a small wedding. Fergie nudged him in the low ribs with her elbow, as if she'd had the same idea.

At the back, behind an altar, a podium stood at the center of the raised stage. A baptismal font was off to the left, so Al figured the pastor's office would be off to the right. In many ways, the church was like the one in which he'd married Abbie oh so many years ago. This place even smelled the same, perhaps because they used the same Murphy Oil Soap to polish the wooden pews. Maury had been the best man on that occasion, and the world would have been a better place if he hadn't eventually tried to prove that. *Old news. Painful news. But old.*

Al almost called out. But it didn't feel right in the quiet church, and the pastor might have been in the middle of a thought about heaven or hell, whatever they talked about these days. He led the way up along the aisle on the far right and headed for an open doorway, where he could see wooden stairs going up a level in two short flights. The church was as still as a mausoleum until they got closer.

At the base of the steps, before he started up, he heard panting. *Gasp. Gasp. Gasp.* At first thought, he figured the pastor was having a heart attack and that he should rush up there. Then he heard a female voice.

"Oh God. Oh God. Oh God."

"Shhh. Keep it quiet."

That second one, a male voice, had to be the preacher's. Al glanced toward Fergie. She had her hand up to her mouth and was struggling to keep from laughing out loud.

They both took a couple of steps back and waited just outside the open doorway leading to the stairs.

Fergie leaned close and whispered to Al, her breath warm on his ear, "I wonder if his wife ever caught him in the middle of doing whatever he's doing up there."

He whispered back. "My guess is she has. That's why she's back there at the house baking up a storm, keeping herself busy."

"Well, if it was me, I'd be sharpening up the knives, and this stuffed shirt would be singing soprano before he knew it."

Time ticked slowly by until Al heard a rustle, and the door to the office opened. A young woman started down the stairs. Her bouncing curly hair, more strawberry blond than red, looked a bit tousled, and she had a few extra pounds on her but a quite pretty pale-white face. She was stuffing the tail of her white blouse, which she'd buttoned wrong, into her red skirt until she spotted Al and Fergie.

"Oh. Have you two been waiting long?" Her casual tone had the rug yanked from under it by the pink then red flush that spread across her round cheeks.

"We were wondering if Pastor Sinders is in," Al said. He'd come within an ace of saying "in the middle of anything."

"Oh. Yes. He's here." One hand made a short wave upward. "We were just... talking."

She hurried past them, and her red high heels clicked as she scurried, nearly breaking into a run as she headed for the front door.

Al knocked at the door.

"Come."

They stepped inside. Sinders sat behind a wide dark executive desk with a matching set of shelves behind it on the wall. He didn't rise or offer to shake hands. Just as well. Al might have been reluctant, and Fergie might well have punched him.

The pastor waved a hand toward two oxblood-leather chairs on the other side of his desk. He had the quick and ready composure of someone unaware that Al and Fergie had been standing just outside as long as they had been.

Al eased into his chair and kept a wary eye on Fergie.

The desk was a big one and didn't have a single scrap of paper on it. The surface was like an aircraft carrier, big enough to lie down on. Sinders bent forward and folded his arms on it. Al didn't care to touch it.

Sinders wore a white shirt without a tie and a dark jacket over that, one that could be Brooks Brothers for all Al could tell. The pastor was in his midforties perhaps, with just an inch or two of grey starting to show at his temples. His hair was swept back from a rectangular face and blue eyes that could be intense, even piercing.

"What brings you here?" Sinders asked. "Thinking of using our cozy little church for your wedding?"

"We're not quite there yet," Al said.

"One of us isn't," Fergie said.

"Though this place does look perfect for a romantic moment," Al said.

"Oh." Sinders frowned for a second. "Then what is it?"

"We're following up on a woman for whom you gave a reference. A Cynthia Standerblum."

Al couldn't be sure, but it seemed for a second Sinders twitched in his chair.

"Really? Now let's see."

"She's a rainmaker," Fergie said. "Helps people raise money for programs, campaigns, that sort of thing."

"I suppose I do recall her, though it's been a while. She helped with a special call we made for the missions. We brought her in especially for it."

"She probably left about the time some money came up missing."

"Now, that turned out to be just an accounting error. All that is cleared up." He put his hands together, the fingers forming a steeple.

He leaned closer, staring at them both, Fergie a little longer. Al didn't look to see if Fergie shuddered.

"So everything was fine, and she did good work. That's why you gave her a hearty recommendation."

"Indeed. That's exactly why."

"Well, I guess that takes care of that." Al stood and nodded to Fergie.

She led the way out the office door.

"Hey, wait. Why did you want to know?"

Al ignored the preacher and kept walking. The guy probably needed to do more research on sin and such.

Five minutes later, Al and Fergie were walking across the parking lot to his truck. He couldn't see steam coming out of her ears but could imagine it.

"That's all we were going to get from him, isn't it?" She slid into her side.

"I think we know what she had on him that kept him from making a stink and even encouraged him to go so far as to give her a recommendation."

"Men." Fergie looked out her side window as Al left the church lot.

Just a few miles down the road, after looking out her side window a spell, her mood shifted. She started humming to herself. Then she sang almost under her breath, "Just a little wedding tune that says there's gonna be a wedding soon."

"I don't think that woman we met on the stairs is going to marry soon," Al said.

"Who says I was talking about her? Besides, you missed the sparkle on her hand of an engagement ring *and* a wedding band."

"Oh, my. Doesn't that tiptoe pretty close to one of the Ten Commandments?" Al asked.

"Hell, it stomps all over it."

Chapter Three

She didn't speak again until they'd gone a couple of miles down the road. "Now what?"

"The only other real contact on the list of recommendations." Al glanced toward her. "You're going to like this one."

"Why?"

"He's a politician."

"Active?"

"Was. But there's a bit of a cloud over him at the moment."

"Let me guess," Fergie said. "There are accusations of sexual harassment about him?"

"Bingo." He waited a few ticks. "You don't have to be along for this one if you don't want to."

"Try and stop me. You're talking about the one on the resume? Senator Ned Bentley?"

"Yep."

"You know, even though Congress is in session, he's taken leave to defend against accusations of sexual harassment, several of them."

"It's getting to be a common theme," Al said. "One that puts him in league with Harvey Weinstein, Anthony Weiner, Bill Cosby, and Penn State's Jerry Sandusky, and let's toss in the various sex-abuse claims within the Catholic Church."

"Not to mention the cozy little church in the woods we just left." Fergie gave an undignified snort. "Bentley claims he is innocent, of course. But films have turned up for at least three of the accusations, and more films and hard evidence may be forthcoming."

"Soon, he'll have enough for a documentary." Al shook his head. "It's kind of hard to put a spin on that and get people to believe he did nothing. What's he doing about all that now?"

"Mostly arm waving and complete denial, from what I've seen. Even his supporters are taking a hit for backing him up. They've begun to distance themselves from him. Three people on his staff have resigned. And his wife, one of the last to leave the sinking ship, has just filed for divorce."

"Well, he's the one we're going to try to see next."

"This just gets better and better."

BENTLEY HAD CHOSEN his getaway cabin with care. Al pulled off the two-lane road onto a winding gravel two-rut road that wove up a hill through thick stands of mountain cedar.

"He certainly has a remote corner of the county for his getaway retreat." Fergie bounced up and down and reached to grab the overhead strap above her door as the truck started up a steeper patch of lane. "Probably keeps the press away while he's trying to have his way with former aides and such."

"I'm betting he has a four-wheel-drive vehicle for this." Al shifted down a gear, and his truck rumbled as it lurched up the lane.

The once-thick green stands of mountain cedar that crowded the way and probably only got trimmed by the passing of vehicles were fading to brown, some already the rusty orange of a dying plant. Deeper-rooted live oaks and pecan trees towered up in the distance. But closer to them, everything seemed to have turned brown except for an occasional patch of prickly-pear cactus. The woods around them held some pretty sickly cedar. Al thought back to the drought years when fires had swept through great chunks of the Texas wilds. Bentley had been plain lucky that the fires hadn't swept through here. The woodsy area around his place was a tinderbox waiting for a spark.

The last quarter of a mile went up an even steeper pitch until the truck surged over onto a more level stretch that led to the cabin, a good thirty yards ahead. Al spotted a wider gravel patch beside the road and pulled over. "Let's walk the rest of the way from here."

"Trying to sneak up on him?"

Al shrugged. He didn't know what to expect. He could see a small white Mercedes C-Class sedan pulled up in front of the cabin, which was paneled with siding meant to look like wood. *The old "Abe Lincoln born in a log cabin" thing.* Al sighed. The roof was covered in steel sheets with raised ribs that had been painted a rust brown to look like terra-cotta.

The place probably had two or three bedrooms and one open center room, on the order of a suite. Big picture windows, with the drapes pulled at the moment, gave the place views out across the rolling hills. Bentley probably owned the hundred nearest acres around, and the next house was a mile or two away. Al envied the man that.

The front of the cabin had been zero landscaped with potted barrel cacti and a lone palo verde tree in a weed-free lawn of pea gravel. The door was a darker reddish brown with a small arc of cut-glass wedges at eye level to act as a peephole of sorts.

Fergie stepped close to knock, since no doorbell was visible.

Before her knuckles touched the wood, Al heard the sound of a quick metal slide and click. Many years had passed since he had been out in the thick of a wartime situation on a front, but he reached for Fergie and slammed her to the ground and fell across her.

"What the bloody hell...?" She struggled to push herself out from under him.

The first of the bullets slapped across the face of the house from left to right. *Wham, wham, wham, wham, wham,* in the seemingly endless close-spaced string an automatic weapon makes. Chips flew from the cabin. Holes punched through at waist level, slicing across the house from one side to the other, as if trying to cut it in half.

After a brief pause, probably to shove another clip into place, the shooting started again.

Fergie quit struggling to push him off. Her hazel eyes opened wide as she looked into his eyes.

"Sounds like an AR-15," he said. "Probably has a bump stock, like that maniac in Las Vegas used. Stores were selling more of them after that, instead of fewer."

"But who?" Fergie asked.

"Maybe Bentley should have checked to see if any of the husbands of those women he defiled had a membership in the NRA."

Glass shattered, and wood chips flew all around them as the shooting continued. Al pressed Fergie closer to the ground and stayed as low as he could get himself.

In the middle of one of the strings of shots slamming into the house, the front door eased open a couple of feet. Al found himself looking into the wide-open eyes of Senator Ned Bentley, who was lying flat on the floor and appeared to be trying to crawl out his front door.

Al's first impression was that even though they were under heavy fire and Bentley's house was being shredded just above their heads, the man had happy eyes. Probably part of the charisma that had gotten him elected and had aided him in seducing a number of women, with or without their permission.

"Are you all the ones shooting at me?" Bentley had the long, slow drawl of someone raised in the Deep South.

Al could smell alcohol, maybe brandy. "Have you been drinking?"

"I've sipped away the better part of a bottle of calvados since breakfast, but I'd hardly call that drinking. Did you know we seem to be under far here?"

Normally, the kind of accent that turned "fire" into "far" amused Al. But he estimated at least a hundred rounds had plowed into the house by now. If the shooter didn't have more than one gun, his barrel was getting pretty hot.

Bentley rolled onto his side and took a good look at Fergie. "You're a perty filly."

"Didn't you just notice we're being shot at?" Fergie asked.

"That doesn't take away from you being perty."

Al bet Fergie was half a breath away from telling the senator her real age. But then, he doubted she would go that far.

She did sigh and give Al an eye roll.

"Get ahold of one end of him," Al told Fergie.

He grabbed Bentley by the upper torso, with a hand under each upper arm, and tugged. Fergie took hold of the man's feet. *Just as well,* Al figured. If she had his end, she might have strangled the guy.

Flames had started to leap up inside the shattered windows of Bentley's cabin as they slithered him across the gravel. They used the cover of the all-wheel-drive Mercedes that had collapsed when its tires had been shot. Staying as low to the ground as he could, Al pulled as Fergie pushed Bentley off into the thick of the woods to the right. He struggled to free himself, but they kept him sliding along until they were at least a hundred yards from the cabin. Al put a hand across the senator's mouth and raised his own head enough to look around.

The cabin was on fire, and the woods around them would soon be too. Bentley struggled. Al pressed harder with his hand, and Fergie sat on him to hold him still.

Al saw a man in camo, still shooting away with one AR-15 at his hip and another slung over his back, run up to the cabin and slip inside. Another man in camo ran in from the other direction and rushed inside. Al nodded to Fergie.

They rose and ran, frog-stepping the senator along until they got to Al's truck. They tossed him into the back seat, and Fergie squeezed in beside him and pressed him low. Al started the truck, swung it around in as tight a turn as he could manage, smashing into some low browning cedar growth on the right, and they were off down the gravel lane in a cloud of white dust and spraying stones as Al kept his foot on the gas even though they were fairly flying along.

Bentley struggled to sit up and catch a glimpse of his getaway cabin, riddled with holes and in flames. "That's what you get when you don't pay your bills on time."

Fergie yanked him back down and may have popped him one in the gut, judging from the "Umph" and quiet after that.

Al didn't see anyone behind him but broke every speeding law he could until he had put ten miles and a couple of random turns into their escape.

Up ahead, a defunct gas station on the corner sat next to a motel that was still open, sometimes, but little used. Al knew a small alley ran along behind them. He slowed enough to ease into the alley and snugged up behind the motel. When he turned off the truck, its inside was as still as Al had ever heard it.

He worked his phone out of his pocket, punched in a number, and got it up to his ear. The dispatcher who answered was new and wouldn't switch him directly to the sheriff.

"Give me Victor Kahlon, then."

She could do that.

When Victor answered, Al said, "Do you know where Senator Ned Bentley's cabin is? Not his house, his retreat."

"Yeah."

"Well, you'd better get every fire department near there to send every unit they can. There's a helluva fire just getting going up there. And advise them there are at least two armed shooters, so you'd better have deputies go in first."

"Where are you?"

"I'm as away from there as I can get. Someone turned his place into Swiss cheese with AR-15s."

"Is he okay?"

"I got him out. I'll update you and write up a statement in a bit. I'm taking him to his city house. You'd best get cracking." Al put his phone away.

"Did either of you get a good look at those jaspers who were shooting at me?" Bentley sat up and looked around. Darned if he wasn't grinning, and his eyes smiled as well. He was like some kid at an amusement park, though he stayed on the other side of the back seat from Fergie, who must have caught him a pretty good one in the ribs.

"Nope. We had just dropped by to ask you about someone else," Al said.

"Who?"

"Cynthia Standerblum."

Bentley's brow furrowed as he thought, probably sorting through who-knew-how-long a string of female faces. "Oh." He brightened. "The rainmaker. What about her? That election's long in the rearview mirror by now."

"You gave her a recommendation," Fergie said. "Why?"

"She did a good job. I ended up with quite a war chest, enough to keep my seat in Congress."

"Didn't a pretty good chunk of money come up missing?" Al asked.

"Well... that sort of thing happens from time to time. A small matter in the scheme of things."

"Her role was just to get you re-elected, then she moved on, right?"

"That's pretty much it."

"She didn't have something on you, something she could hold over your head?" Fergie leaned closer.

Bentley glanced toward the door, perhaps measuring his chances of getting out of the truck before she popped him again. Some of the playfulness left his face. Maybe he was sobering enough to realize he had just about been killed back there and probably would have been if Al and Fergie hadn't come along.

"She was a Texas gal," Bentley said, "like myself."

Al caught Fergie grinning in spite of herself.

Perhaps realizing how awkward he'd sounded, Bentley said, "I gave her a reference. Let's leave it at that."

"I know the Secret Service doesn't usually protect senators, but if you explain what happened back at that cabin, maybe they will."

"I may not mention it."

"You've swept enough under the rug," Fergie said.

"I don't think you have a choice," Al said. "I imagine every unit from every nearby fire station is on their way to the scene to keep the whole woods from going up and spreading across the county. The deputies who go in first will probably notice the odd bullet hole in the charred remains of anything left of the cabin, not to mention the way your car looks. You heard me give the department a heads-up about the shooters."

"I've talked my way out of worse pickles. Do you think they'll find out who was shooting at me?"

"You don't have any ideas yourself about who might be that riled and heavily armed?" Al said.

"Oh, there are a number of people who have taken umbrage to me lately. It's why I was taking a few days to relax in the peace and quiet away from it all," Bentley said.

"Well, so much for peace and quiet," Fergie said.

A SHERIFF'S DEPARTMENT cruiser and two Westlake Police cars were parked in a row in front of the senator's main house, a McMansion in suburban Westlake. Westlake was an upscale suburb on the west side of Austin. It took money to live there, and most years, the high-school football team played like semipros. Bentley's yard looked professionally landscaped. The lawn was as neatly mowed as a golf course and looked a bright green in spite of the current drought and citywide water restrictions. Al almost asked if Bentley's wife was home then caught himself in time. Bentley had mentioned having a chauffeur who also acted as bodyguard. But he was going to need more than that.

Victor Kahlon climbed out of the sheriff's department cruiser.

"How come you're not out at the fire?" Al asked.

"Clayton sent our SWAT unit in first. They've given an 'all clear,' and the fire departments are doing what they can to keep half the county from going up in smoke."

"I'll bet that's putting a knot in Clayton's undies," Al said.

"He did seem a touch miffed. He claims he'd given you something entirely different to attend to."

"This just came up along the way there." Al turned to the senator. "You'll have to give a statement, and if I were you, I'd tell things exactly as they happened. They'll be checking what you say against the statements Fergie and I will make."

"You're not coming right to the department?" Victor asked.

"Nope. I still have Clayton's chore to tend to. We don't want to disappoint him, now do we?" Al got back into his truck.

As Bentley walked up to his front door, a Westlake cop on either side, Fergie climbed into the front passenger seat. She gave an unladylike spit out onto the curb. "He's supposed to be so damned charming."

"You speak for half the women in America," Al said. "But I imagine all that will get sorted out in a courtroom somewhere."

"It's not even noon yet. What do we do now in what has already turned into a charming day?" Fergie gave him a raised eyebrow.

"I guess now we have to go through the motions and take a look around for that damned chupacabra."

LEE FENSTON RAN DOWN the slope as fast as his legs could carry him, the steep pitch of the hill and the growing wall of flames behind him helping speed him along.

Garson McBallister burst into view from the other downward-sloping side of the hill as they both approached the boosted Cherokee they had parked down by the main road earlier.

Lee started the engine and looked around. For a minute, he thought they might have to leave Brandon Highwater behind. He kind of wished they could except the guy could identify them. They'd come across him in the woods a couple days back when they were scouting Bentley's getaway place. That didn't make Brandon one of them, though he'd had the same misfortune to have a pretty wife who worked within the spell of Senator Bentley that they both had. He also had some backwoods experience he thought made him a regular Davy fucking Crockett, nothing like their serious military backgrounds. He hadn't been much help yet, but he hadn't gotten in the way either. Now he was running behind.

Lee had short blond hair and cheek stubble that matched. A scar he was rather proud of ran from the outside corner of his left eye and went down almost to his throat. His pride came from how very close the cut had come to killing him. But the other guy was the one who'd died.

Garson's hair was cut so short that his head looked shaved, with just a shading of black where he would have had a full head of hair if he cared. He always looked intense enough to be wearing a permanent squint.

Lee kept looking all around them with rapid jerks of his head. Just as he was ready to shift into gear, Brandon came legging it toward them, pushing through a thicket of black persimmon and sumac bushes. He was trying to look in three directions at once as he ran.

He swung the back door open and slid in with his deer rifle across his lap. "Okay. We can go."

"Where were you?" Garson asked.

"I followed the ones whisking Bentley away, tried to get a shot."

"Did you?"

"Nope. They stayed low and were gone in a flash."

"Did you know them?"

"I didn't even see them that clearly. I just know there were two of them, that they had Bentley with them, and that they had a truck."

Lee eased up closer to the road. As soon as it looked clear in both directions, he shot the Cherokee out from behind its cover and started down the road as though they were folks just out having a regular day. He kept a close eye on the rearview mirror for anyone who might have spotted them as well as a lookout ahead for any roadblocks. He felt it was odds against for either, but he had gotten way beyond wary during multiple tours of both Iraq and Afghanistan. *Too soon for roadblocks.* Fire trucks were still screaming by them, going the other way. A few minutes later, that changed to sheriff's department cruisers. None of them paid any attention to the vehicle Lee was driving.

"Do you think those two got a good look at us?" Lee asked Garson.

"I don't know." Garson looked out at the brownish countryside going by. "I never saw them in the first damned place. You only told me we'd had company when we were getting clear of there after we found no one home."

"Bentley was home, all right. They got him out of there, whoever they are. I just want to know if they saw you."

"Dammit. I said we should have gotten masks first."

"In this heat?"

"We've been to a helluva lot hotter places than this," Garson said.

"Well, first things first. We know where that bastard Bentley lives. We can only hope he's stupid and stubborn enough to go there instead of to some safe house."

"I know where a couple of those are too if it comes to that," Garson said.

"Knowing this guy, a scare will likely send him to the regular place where he feels comfy and safe, like a rabbit to its hole."

"And where the liquor cabinet is stocked the way he likes it."

"I got the license number of the truck," Brandon Highwater said.

Lee glanced toward Garson, who stayed fixed on whatever was going by out the side window.

"I have a cousin who works at the DMV." Brandon leaned forward. "I'll know today who was in that truck that got him out of there. Don't you worry. If you want, I'll tend to them while you go after Bentley."

"When we get their names, why don't you go and keep an eye on them for us. Okay? Let us know if they still have Bentley with them," Lee said.

Garson turned his head to look at him. Lee gave him a slow wink.

"Yeah, just that. An eye only." Garson went back to looking out his side window.

Lee shook his head. They would have to deal with those other two after they took care of Bentley. They hadn't figured out just what to do with Brandon.

"Yeah, that'll be a big help," Lee said. "A really big help."

Chapter Four

Fergie kept an eye on Al as he drove. This was very like him, to be grumping at one moment about wishing to stay at home and sleep in, the next to be off like an engine racing.

These little outings almost always ended up with someone shooting at them. He had to be delighted with that, like hot sauce poured into his chili.

His eyes shone brightly as he gripped the wheel firmly. "I know a little place up ahead."

He turned his head toward her, and darned if he didn't wink.

The "place" turned out to be a mom-and-pop general store on the corner of an intersection of a couple of two-lane roads. He pulled up into one of several empty parking spots by the front door. He hopped out his side. She figured she'd better get a wiggle on and got out too.

Inside in the dimly lit interior, her eyes were drawn to merchandise on shelves piled to the ceiling, where an overhead fan lumbered slowly round and round. The organization of everything felt loose. Fishing tackle was stacked next to paper products. Canned soups sat right beside containers of motor oil.

Still, something smelled good. Two tables covered in red-and-white checkered cloths were off to one side. She recalled seeing a sign outside proclaiming that worms for fishing were available.

They sat down at one of the tables just as a white-haired woman stuck her head out from between curtains that covered the way to some back room.

"What'll it be, Al? By land or by sea?"

"Sea," he said.

The head disappeared.

Al must have seen the unasked question on her face. "This time of day, she only serves chicken-fried steak or catfish. I ordered us the catfish and chips. That okay?"

"Sure. Sure. You've eaten here before?"

"Many times."

She envied him that, his years as a deputy where he got to rove all over the county while she had patrolled within the confines of the city. Even by the time they'd both moved up to do detection work, he still was out in nature much of the time. Most years weren't as dry and crispy as this one was turning out to be.

The lady, wearing a blue denim apron, came out carrying two gigantic glasses of iced tea.

"Thanks, El," Al said.

Fergie could see the name now, Elodie, embroidered on the taupe name patch on her apron.

"That's a pretty name," Fergie said.

The woman grinned, revealing one gold upper tooth.

"It's a French form of Alodia," Al said. "Comes from the German phrase for 'foreign riches.'"

"Isn't he just a pip?" Elodie headed back toward what Fergie had figured out was the kitchen, behind those curtains.

"Have you heard anything about a chupacabra, El?" Al asked.

She paused and turned her head to look back at him. "Oh, land yes. You haven't been talking to those goat people, have you?"

"I'm about to. We're fixing to pay a call on a Flora-Ida Bruntz."

"Well, you'd best button your wallet pocket. I hear tell her kin go all the way back to gypsies." Elodie chuckled to herself as she disappeared into the curtain.

"This part of the county has its fair share of goats." Al squeezed his lemon wedge into his glass of tea and took a sip. "There're also small cattle spreads and a horse ranch or two. But one darn lot of goats."

"I never had an idea Texas had so many goats, and I've lived here all my life." She was sorry as soon as she said it.

"Texas heads the nation in goat population," he said, "with over a million. That's half the goat population of all the states. Nothing like cattle, though. We also lead in that, with over eleven million steers."

She'd done it to herself, gotten him started. She wondered sometimes if he had ever forgotten a single thing he had learned. Worse was his tendency to share, in great detail, his erudition of such trivia.

She was looking around the merchandise-cluttered room for something to change the subject when Elodie came out, carrying two heaping baskets of deep-fried catfish and home country fries. One finger curled around the neck of a bottle of ketchup, which she plunked down onto the table as well.

After she had scurried back out of sight, Fergie said, "This is okay this once, but we're having salad for supper, right?"

"Yes, dear."

The catfish was exceptional, though, and she made herself stop halfway through, although her taste buds pulled her forward. She ate only a few of the fries despite their spicy crispness. If she ate this way every day, she'd be as round as a bowling ball. She started to hope they would do something in the afternoon to burn some energy, although it would be hard to top dragging a senator across a leaf-crackling woods floor under a hail of bullets.

By the time they left the little store, midafternoon had settled in with scorching heat, and still not a cloud in the sky.

Al pulled out his cell phone while the AC roared as it brought the truck interior to a livable temperature. "Yeah, Victor. It's me. What's the word on that fire?"

When he got a reply, he turned to Fergie. "They have it under control."

Back into the phone, he asked, "How about the shooters in camo?"

He shook his head at the reply. "Sure. We'll be in to do our statements. Right now, we're off on that merry chore Clayton had for us. Tell him that's what's keeping us busy, if he asks."

Chapter Five

Fergie rolled down her window for a moment. A blast of oven-hot air swept across her. She rolled it back up. Al was pulling into the lane of a ranch with a sign that said Boer Goats.

She nearly asked about Boer goats but caught herself just in time. She'd already endured a brief information dump about the population of goats in Texas.

"Boer means farmer in Dutch, and the farmers were in South Africa. I'm told Boer goats have only been in Texas since 1993 but do well against the heat and disease."

Al stopped just in time. He probably hadn't heard her teeth grinding but had almost certainly registered the large, labored sigh.

She'd never been on a goat ranch of this scale before. The fencing was different from a cattle or horse ranch. This wire fence was high enough to keep them from jumping over, and the squares were small enough to keep them from sticking their heads through, though some seemed determined to try. A number of them ran along beside Al's truck as he went up the drive. Far more ignored the truck entirely, going about their eating or climbing up onto any object they could.

All the large trees had been nibbled at as high as the goats could reach, in the aptly named process of "goating" a tree.

Bales of hay, feeding troughs, and livestock watering troughs dotted the wide-open fields. Small open sheds with slanting roofs gave the goats a place to get out of the rain or harshest sun. Many of the goats were crowded in the shade of those.

Ahead, a ranch house and what looked like more housing for goats sprawled across a hill. Al pulled the truck to a stop in the loop that swung past the front door.

They got out and were halfway to the front door when Al said, "Hold up a moment."

She looked where he was staring. A woman came over a slight hill with goats crowded around her like a cloud. Fergie's first impression came from the clothes: bright yellow, blue, and red in the blouse above a red skirt over rubber galoshes that went up high enough to disappear under the skirt. She carried two large white buckets. As she got closer, Fergie caught the glitter of round metal disks and coins sewn to the upper part of the shirt. Fergie had seen shirts that brightly colored worn by the Seminole Indians of Florida, but this was the first Texan woman she'd seen so attired.

They stood and waited until she came through a gate, pushing the goats back until she could get through. She came toward them, smiling. Her hair was a dark brown, almost black, with wisps of grey just starting to show at her temples. Her skin was tanned saddle-leather brown by the sun. Her face showed obvious laugh wrinkles, and her brown eyes glittered, already in on something funny although she hadn't yet been introduced.

"So you're the sorry lot the sheriff sent?" She chuckled, putting her buckets down, then held out a hand.

Fergie had to fight against wincing at a raspy-palmed handshake so firm that it made Fergie want to look at her hand when the woman let go.

"You're Flora-Ida Bruntz?" Al must have braced against the handshake of someone who labored on a farm. He matched the woman's smile.

"The one and only. Accept no substitutes." She must have caught a slight quizzical tilt to Fergie's head. "Why don't we sit down somewheres and have a lemonade. I take it this is your first visit to a goat farm."

"Yep. I was a city detective, while Al here worked the county. So he knows a bit more about goats."

"Retired, eh? Figures that sheriff would send out his best."

"Well, Al here—"

"I'm just joshin' ya, honey. Any help's a step forward over being ignored."

She led them around the side of the ranch house to a flagstone patio. She waved to a glass-topped table under an umbrella. She put her buckets down outside the back door before slipping into the house.

"Doesn't smell too bad," Fergie said. "I don't mind horse ranches and have gotten used to cattle spreads. But I'm catching hardly a whiff here."

"That's miles above being around Meat Jenkins at his place."

"Don't even get me started."

Flora-Ida came out the door, nudging it to one side with her hip while she carried a tray with a pitcher of lemonade and glasses.

She poured them each a glass and sat down. "Truth be told, I'm always glad for a break. Nothing can be more doting than a herd of goats, but their enthusiasm rarely lets up."

"I get the feeling you haven't been in Texas long," Al said. "How long have you been goat farming here?"

"Just a few years. No one told me it would be like living on a skillet."

"It isn't always this hot, or this dry, if that helps. Though I doubt it does," Fergie said. "Why Texas, and why goats?"

"I had kin here who helped me get a start." She took a hearty sip of her lemonade.

"Do you mind if we cut to the chase?" Al took a sip of his lemonade, lowered the glass, and looked at Fergie, who had just taken her first sip.

"Do you always put tequila in your lemonade?" he asked.

"You don't?"

"Anyway, the chupacabra," Al said. "Have you seen it?"

She shook her head. "Few have."

"Then how do you know there is one?"

"When you find two, maybe three goats with their blood drained out from holes in their necks, laying there stiff with flies buzzing about in the morning, then you have to assume it's not a giant bat or the neighbor's eleven-year-old doing that in the night."

"But you've never really seen one?" Fergie asked.

"You've gotta understand. I was a skeptic myself at first. It made as much sense as cow tipping. But I've got something."

The goat lady dug into a pocket at the side of her skirt and brought out a cell phone. She flipped through a few pictures until she found what she wanted. She passed the phone over to Fergie. Al crowded close to look too.

The image wasn't blurry, nor did it look photoshopped. An animal was stretched out on the ground on its side in one photo, and its body had been propped up to face the camera in the next.

"I'd heard that they might just be coyotes with mange, but I'd be hard pressed to say that's what this is," Al said.

The creature was mostly hairless and had a grey body roughly the size of a large coyote. But that's where the comparison ended for Fergie. Its pointed drooping ears had a tuft of hair here and there, but the body and face were covered by wrinkles and wart-like bumps. Its eyes were a blank white, and the mouth was frozen open in a snarl of some of the most misshapen and gnarly teeth she had ever seen. Gackle-toothed, she might say. It looked like nothing she would care to run into in the night. It looked more like something that had staggered out of the wrong end of a nuclear plant.

"A friend sent the picture after they killed this... *thing* on their goat ranch. Their goats had been killed the same way as mine, throats ripped, blood drained."

"So you believe this thing actually exists?" Fergie asked.

"What I believe is my goats are dead in the morning, and I want to know what's doing it. Is there anything you can do?" Her tone suggested she was bracing herself for a no, which she had probably heard from others so far.

Fergie glanced toward Al, waiting.

"I'll tell you what I'll do." Al pushed his glass of so-called lemonade an inch farther away with one finger. "I'm going to ask the sheriff's department to send over one of their animal control people to set up two or three of those wildlife night-vision cameras and place them where you think you're getting any traffic from this creature. They usually fix them to a tree or pole, and any unwanted animal motion at night will start them recording. That way you'll at least perhaps get peace of mind about what's doing this."

"Oh my God." She leaned back in her chair and stared at him. "You really believe me. Well, you're the first."

Al wiggled the fingers of one hand. "Not to worry."

Fergie was as surprised as the goat lady. She waited to see what Al was up to.

"I'll tell you another thing... for free. If I were you, I'd go to one of the local pet shelters and see about adopting a livestock guard dog or two. I know most of the rescue places real well and would be glad to put in a word for you."

"I... I don't know what to say."

"Or I'll tell you what you could do that's even better than that, what many Texas sheep and goat ranchers do. Go get yourself a jenny mule or donkey, a good-sized one, maybe five hundred pounds or so and around forty-eight inches at the withers. A jenny is better than a jack since they tend to be more maternal. Get an older one that's outgrown her playfulness. They're naturally aggressive toward canines and coyotes in particular. If yours comes across a chupacabra, she's liable to apply her back heels to it and kick it into the next county. You only need hope you get the encounter on film with one of your cameras if you plan to get anything like points for a field goal."

Flora-Ida tilted her head. "Are you having fun with me at my expense?"

"No. It's true. I should have thought of it," Fergie said. "Even though I was a city cop for my years, I've at least heard of that."

Al nodded. "Also, you only need one per pasture, not two or three. That way, it will socialize with your goats better. A jenny with a foal is even better since its defense mode is in full alert. The foal will turn into a good guard animal too when it's grown. And when the jenny is charging or attacking, stay the hell away from her. Afterwards, give her time to calm down before you get near her."

The goat lady's eyes were open wide now. "I will tell you one thing for true. I didn't expect anyone to be this helpful. My uncle didn't tell me any of this when he helped me get started. I'll do what you say. And I'll look forward to that fella with the cameras. Now, you let me know if there's anything I can do for you."

One woman to another, Fergie found Flora-Ida a bit of an enigma. One side of her, the Gypsy side perhaps, seemed clever and quite capable. The other side possessed a farm-girl innocence, which Fergie found refreshing, though it made her the sort who might believe in a chupacabra. A quite different aspect of the situation that struck Fergie was how Al dealt with the woman's complexity. He was kind, attentive, and respectful—not as some kind of act but in a sincere way that helped Fergie understand why he worked so well interacting with so many people in the county. He was one of them.

"Well, there is one thing," Al said. "I was wondering if you happen to know anyone high up in the rankings of any gypsies in Texas."

Her face beamed, and she nodded. "My Uncle Mo, who helped set me up here, is sort of what you folk would call the King of Texas Gypsies."

Aha. Fergie thought Al had perked up and gotten a glitter in his eyes back when Elodia had been serving them lunch and mentioned gypsies. Now, she was getting an inkling why he had brightened up then and was being so accommodating to Flora-Ida now. That old chess player inside him was a move ahead of Fergie once again.

AL'S CELL PHONE RANG. He glanced at the screen, frowned, and pulled over to the side of the road to take the call.

"Go ahead. It's your dime."

"You know who this is?"

"Yeah, a US senator whose fat we only recently pulled from the fire, literally, and from whom we never got so much as a thank-you. What do you want?"

"Look. I'm sorry about that. I was rattled."

"You were swizzled."

"That too."

Al waited.

"Sheriff Clayton told me who you are, a retired county detective. He said you were pretty capable and had done some amazing things."

"And?"

"I'd like to hire you for protection."

"I'm more of a 'find things out' sort of guy, not a 'take a bullet for the boss' sort. I suggest you put in a call to the feds. I'm sure after what you've been through, they might decide to give you some free protection."

"I'm afraid it isn't going to be enough."

"I don't know how I could do anything they can't do."

"But—"

"I'm not your man." Al hung up.

LEE CAME OUT OF THE Banana Arms military surplus store and squinted up at the relentless sun.

Garson nearly bumped into him from behind. "We might could have picked up a couple of those Aussie sun hats as well."

"Most of what we'll be doing will be in the dark," Lee said. "Besides, I never cared for the way the brim attaches up on one side."

"Not all of them do that or have to do that," Garson said.

High in a hackberry tree they passed, a grackle that looked as big and black as a raven gave a loud crackling screech. Lee looked past the tree into the glare of the sun's growing heat and thought twice about those Aussie hats.

"Bentley's name sure made the radio news," he said.

Garson nodded. "Won't help him get reelected, no matter how much sympathy the public has about a fire at his place in the woods."

"But it did let us know where he's holed up."

"And there was no mention of who caused that fire," Garson said.

"We've still got a cleanup job to do, and let's hope it's not another messy one."

Garson shrugged.

"Now, about these witnesses..." Lee looked around, never ever fully at ease.

"Let's see what that Brandon guy has found," Garson said.

Brandon sat on the lowered tailgate of his truck, grinning like a kid going to the fair. He was close to their age. Maybe that had to do with the age their wives were, whatever attracted Bentley. But they thought of him as younger. Their tours of duty had aged them inside, toughening them to a point few civilians ever reached.

"I got it," Brandon said. "The truck belongs to some guy named Allard Quinn."

"Well, thanks. That's very helpful." Lee took the piece of paper Brandon held out. He made sure the address was there too.

"You said you were cool with keeping an eye on this Quinn guy, now that we know about him?" Garson asked.

Brandon nodded a little too eagerly.

"Just watch. You hear?" Lee squinted at him.

"You sure you don't need help first with Bentley?"

"What you're helping us with is just as important."

Brandon gave another eager, maybe overeager, nod. He went around and climbed into his truck and took off.

"You think he'll leave this alone?" Garson asked.

"I hope he will. I don't mind risking our necks, but he's such a tender rube."

"Do you think about us dying?"

"When we were in counseling, Brenda and I, back while there was still a dim ray of hope, the therapist said I might have a death wish."

"Do you?" Garson turned to look hard at him.

"I don't know." Lee shook his head. "Maybe I just don't care much one way or the other right now."

"Maybe we scared Bentley enough," Garson said. "Maybe we don't need to do this thing. The public knows now."

"The public ain't gonna do anything, though. We've both seen that before."

"Yeah, you're probably right. It's up to us."

Chapter Six

Al's cell phone rang again. He picked it up, looked around at the traffic on the highway around him, and answered the call.

"It's Victor Kahlon here. Are you surprised to hear from me?"

"Not at all. I expected it."

"As you can imagine, the sheriff is giving me a hot foot to get your statements. Are you close?"

"Sort of." Al glanced at the Welcome to Fredericksburg sign to the right.

"Not at the far end of the county, are you?"

"Sort of." He and Fergie were a couple of counties away from Travis County.

"The thing is, a couple of Secret Service agents are on their way to stay with Senator Bentley and keep an eye on him. They're pretty insistent about seeing your statements since you were right there. The senator wasn't all the way articulate. He claims he was rattled, being under fire and all."

"He was rattled all right." Al could have added that a bottle of apple brandy had done most of the maraca shaking there.

"When can we expect...?"

"We'll have a statement headed your way within the hour. Will that do?"

"Make it happen. Thanks, Al."

Al hung up.

"We have a choice between the Busy Bee Business Center and the local UPS Store." Fergie looked up from the screen of her phone.

"Nothing against the efficiency of a UPS store, but I like the sound of the Busy Bee. We have an hour and a half before meeting up with Flora-Ida's Uncle Mo, and we might as well spend it articulating our fun time in the woods instead of walking around with all the tourists peeking into the shop windows and smelling the flowers in the Market Square."

They both had years of experience with crime-scene statements, so Fergie hovered over Al's shoulder as he sat at a computer at the Busy Bee and tapped out everything helpful they could remember. Once the shooting had broken out, time had fairly zipped along. But they surprised each other about details they recalled in sharp clarity, everything except the faces or anything else about the men in camo they'd seen approaching the flaming cabin. They included Bentley's feeble attempt to hit on Fergie even while they were under fire. Al didn't figure that would do the senator any more damage than had already been done, but it wouldn't help him either.

With the transcription fired off to Vincent, they stepped outside into the nearly one o'clock afternoon heat, so intense that passing trucks sent waves of heat sweeping up across the sidewalk and past them.

They wove through the many tourists still braving the intensity of the day and fighting it with ice cream cones and plastic glasses of beer. Carrying a beer through the Germanic town was both legal and expected. The right, or privilege, was probably how some women got their husbands to come along for a day of browsing through the many craft and novelty shops.

"Here we are." Al pushed open the door of the Fredericksburg Brewing Company.

The inside was always a happy sight for him. Tables to the left held families and groups. In the back, a beer garden, or *biergarten*, had its own crowd of folks at picnic tables.

Al's eyes swept to the right, where a bar with high chairs and then a few stone tables stuck out from one long stone bar just beneath the tall silver fermentation tanks. Those were Al's favorite places to sit.

"Have you spotted him?" Fergie asked.

"That about has to be him." Al nodded toward a man in a three-piece suit, an alpine hat, and a huge white Santalike beard.

As they moved closer, Al could see the suit was a dark-blue tweed with Donegal flecks and had almost certainly been tailored. How someone could wear an outfit like that on a day that could melt the eyelashes off a camel was beyond Al.

But the man was fighting the heat in his own way, with a fluted glass of champagne, a bowl of strawberries, and the bottle in a bucket of ice beside it. He looked up, saw them, and waved a hand to the empty stools at the stone table with a rounded end.

"I had a devil of a time saving seats, what with this crowd, but they know me here and obliged me. And all this bother for a couple of 'gorgers' like yourselves."

But he smiled as he said it, and they sat down.

"You're Flora-Ida's Uncle Mo?" Al asked.

"My real name is Maurice, but who cares for a handle like that?"

"My brother's name is Maurice, but we call him Maury," Al said.

"Wise choice." He turned to Fergie and gave her a flirtish smile as he held out a hand. "And how did a fine young woman like you ever come to work for the likes of the nasty police?"

"I... I..."

"No need to explain," Mo said. "I knew you both were cops, or had been cops, the moment I lamped you. A Rom like me knows these things, needs to know them."

Up close, Al could see that Mo's suit was by no means new. The tweed had a shine in places, and in some spots, small repairs had been made—good ones, but the suit had nevertheless had a long life. Yet it looked quite good from a few steps back, and Mo had chosen to wear it on one blister of a day. The air in the brewery was cooler than most air conditioning, though, so Al guessed it all worked out for Mo.

A waiter in a white shirt with red arm bands came up, and Al ordered a couple of porters.

As soon as the waiter had scurried off, Mo said, "I'm just glad you looked in on little Flora-Ida. She says you're helping and gave her some tooting good advice as well. She's still coming to grips with being a settled person. Most of we Roms are on the move, the go, go, go."

Mo reached for his stemmed glass and took a small sip, looking at them both over the rim. "I keep an eye out for Flora-Ida, helped her get her goats going. She's a bit 'on the shelf' at her age and probably won't have a chance to marry, so she might as well have goats. You see?"

Al nodded. Gypsy girls had once been married off when very young, in their early teens.

The waiter set down two pint glasses of dark-brown porter. Al bought a second or two by taking a sip.

"There's something you're wanting, isn't it?" Mo asked. "You helped her, now you crave something."

"You mentioned 'gorgers.' What does that mean?" Al asked.

Mo's grin showed from behind his beard as well as sparkled in his eyes. "Any non-Gypsy is a mark, a prospective revenue stream waiting to happen."

"I appreciate your candor," Al said.

Mo finished topping off his flute with champagne from the bottle. He reached for a strawberry then shrugged. "You were cops. You've probably heard it all. I promised my niece I'd give you a hand so long as it doesn't cross a line."

Al had a hunch what that line was. "The person we're seeking isn't a Rom," he said.

Mo took a drink from his glass and smacked his lips. "Yep. That's the line."

"The person we seek is a woman, a rainmaker, who took advantage of a hospital's charity raising money for cancer," Al said.

Mo nodded.

"We think she's probably somewhere in Texas."

"Why so?" Mo asked. "If it was me, I'd be off in Maine or someplace as far away."

"A person she worked with said she was a Texas gal. I think she'll be in the state somewhere. Her roots are here. She'll probably be looking for some new scam. Do you know where the opportunities are?"

Mo grinned, popped a strawberry into his mouth, and reached for his glass. After he'd taken a sip he said, "Oh, my. You are indeed in ripe times."

"How so?"

"Well, you've just had a whopper of a hurricane in Texas. Surely, you've been hustled for donations toward that, seen events, heard of local drives to help out. How much of that loose, untraceable money do you think makes it into the hands of anyone needing it for hurricane relief?"

"Not all of it?" Fergie asked.

"I'd be very surprised if as much as half ever does any good." Mo shook his head. "And that doesn't include the motels and gas stations that price gouged. Or the crews that sweep through, putting on new roofs. You pay for thirty-year shingles and get ten-year ones instead, if the job gets done at all and the crew doesn't just skip with any advance money. Most do stay to do the job, though, since they make more that way. I know. I've run that one myself."

"So we should look where the money is loose and fast, right?"

"Don't forget your senior-care centers."

"Really?" Fergie said.

"No one is more gullible. Those residents are at the age when hope is a living thing that can be manipulated. They're saps. You know, people your age."

Al and Fergie glanced at each other.

"You mentioned rainmaking. I tried my hand at that for a spell." Mo rested his hands on his rounded middle. "I don't mean rounding up money, the way you meant it. I mean firing up a plane and releasing flares of silver iodide and calcium chloride particles into clouds to enhance the chances of rain. If there were no clouds, like today, you build a big fire and seed the smoke."

"But you don't think that works?"

"Hell no, or they'd be doing that to put out forest fires. Even the best cloud seeders know you can't break droughts, you can just enhance conditions that already might be ready to bring rain."

"So you did it just as a scam, right?" Fergie said.

He grinned. "And if it rained, I took credit for it. If it didn't, I kept my feet moving but cashed their check anyways. Sounds like your grifter knew when to move on as well."

"She did at that," Al said. "We have a suspicion she'll keep her hand in at some fraud or other, probably a different one. We just don't know what yet."

"I'm guessing your grifter isn't suited for the high-tech opportunities to be had these days, like phishing, hacking, or identity theft."

Al shook his head. He took a sip of his porter. *Gosh, this is good.* "If you had to go to one place where you could dip your toe in a number of possibilities for someone like her to get a new start, is there somewhere like that a person could go?"

Mo shared his biggest grin so far. "Indeed there is. But, remember, you didn't hear anything about it from me."

Al waited, seeking not to look to overeager.

"There's a guy. He runs a kind of camp, a training camp. You could call it a school for scams."

"Really?" Al couldn't help himself.

"Think of it. If you're a really good grifter but don't want to ever get caught, or maybe you're getting on and don't think you could do hard time, why not train others in your craft? It's no risk, and you can live off the tuition. Live nice and safely."

"And there's someone like this?"

Mo nodded and reached for a strawberry. "You're welcome to a strawberry, but I'm told they don't pair well with porter."

"I don't imagine they would," Al said. "Who is this guy?"

"His name is Harley Ray Luther, but some refer to him as the Ghost Cloud because he used to flow through an area and there would be less money when he left than when he arrived. But now, he's a settled person himself, and having a school is a low-risk way of keeping his hand in the till."

"Just where has he settled?"

"In a little town called Armadillo Springs, some eighty to ninety miles northwest of here."

"Would you go there if you were seeking to start over fresh at some different scam or grift?" Al asked.

"I would if I was desperate enough and needed a new identity, a complete package. The ol' Ghost Cloud is your guy for that, all right. A lot of people who are into the same thing, frauds and scams, know each other. Ol' Harley has been known to shelter some of them as they refresh their identities and lay low in general for a spell after a score. He makes money from that or puts them to work in his school."

"So you think that's a good place to look for our missing rainmaker?"

"It's where I would go to start looking." He reached for a strawberry and dropped it into his half glass of champagne. He watched the bubbles rush up around it.

"I'm curious about one thing," Fergie said. "Why give up his name?"

"First of all," Mo said, "because he's not one of us."

"And secondly?"

"He skinned me out of well over a hundred thousand dollars once, when I was younger, much younger. It's another reason I agreed to talk to you at all. I don't care to go after him myself, but I wouldn't mind much if he fell down the stairs... and fell real hard."

When Fergie and Al stood, they made it halfway to the door before Al stopped and went back to the table. He leaned down closer to Mo. "Are you really the King of Texas Gypsies?"

"Hmm. That's rather in my niece's head. She thinks so. And, in truth, I don't discourage her of it. I deem it an affection. But we're really a kingless lot. Some of us have just outlasted the others. Seen to our health better, we have."

As Al turned to walk away, Mo reached to pour more champagne into his glass.

Chapter Seven

Al was chuckling to himself as he wove through the thicker tourist traffic toward the edge of town.

"What?" Fergie asked.

"That Mo."

"What about him?"

"He's quite unabashed about who and what he is. Good for him."

"But there's something else, isn't there?"

"He *knows* things, and I think he knows a lot more than he was going to share with the likes of us."

"Yet he dangled the piece of red yarn in front of the cat."

"He's a manipulator. That's what he does. Maybe telling us outright wouldn't be any fun for someone like that."

"I'm betting too that he has plenty enough money to buy a newer and different suit," Fergie said, "but that one he was wearing is a kind of uniform for when he's in character."

"You won't get an argument from me. Short of the River Walk section in the heart of San Antonio, you'd be pressed to find a spot where the ebb and flow of fresh tourists could be so many marks to someone like him. You could see his eyes sweeping over the crowd in the brewery and sorting them out like a cherry farmer at picking season."

Fergie noticed that Al had headed north out of Fredericksburg instead of back toward his place. "You aren't thinking of heading up to Armadillo Springs to have a look at this Harley Ray Luther, are you?"

Al glanced around at the sky. It did seem to be growing darker. "Well, I—"

His cell phone rang. He picked it up and glanced to see who was calling.

"Oh my."

"Who is it?" Fergie asked.

"Clayton himself." Al pressed the button. "Yes?"

"I'm calling you myself so you don't hear it on the news."

"Hear what?"

"Someone set fire to Bentley's home, the one in the city."

"Oh?"

"Like the tomfool he is, he came running outside, with two Secret Service agents trying to keep him covered."

"You said 'trying.' Why?"

"Because someone took him out, right there between them. They wounded his bodyguard in the process too."

"But left the Secret Service agents alone, right? I guess the shooter's quarrel wasn't with them."

"We think not. They agree."

"If their job was to protect him, they pretty well failed at that."

"They're upset about that too. Their boss, as well as Austin's FBI agent in charge, Benjamin Omar Bradley, are in a lather to bring in the shooter."

"I'm curious why you called me to tell me all this."

"Because you and your lanky redhead sidekick were eyeball witnesses at the cabin shooting—might have even seen a face. So you're one of several leads the Bureau is following."

"If either of us had seen a face, we'd have put that in our statement."

"The shooter doesn't know that."

"Do they have even the foggiest who the shooter might be?"

"After the fact, Bradley did share his suspicions with me. Those boys work pretty much the same way we do when we're putting together a list of suspects in a situation like this. As high profile as this is, Bradley has alerted all the state and local law-enforcement groups and has several teams himself out scouring for anything that can give them quick traction."

"Doesn't he have anything better than 'Be on the lookout' and scrambling about?"

Clayton chuckled. "Yep. He has a hunch or two. The senator was political, so he had enemies enough, but he was also a player. So in just one direction Bradley took, he considered all the women who had made accusations and complaints against Bentley, and he and his teams took another close look at their husbands. No one got a good look at anyone in the Westlake shooting, but you two saw a couple of men at the senator's cabin. So were any of the husbands particularly mad, missing now, and possessing the needed skills? It seems a couple of the husbands of the women Bentley allegedly abused have military backgrounds."

"I'm betting this is the part where it gets juicy."

"You'd win that bet. One is former Special Ops. The other is a Navy SEAL who happens to be AWOL. The feds are seeking both of them. They've made themselves scarce. They might even be working together on this."

"And they're dangerous?"

"Very."

"So you and the feds think these guys or whoever it is might come after Fergie and me?"

"Correct. They may have seen you, even gotten the license number of your truck. Either of them has excellent tracking skills and, incidentally, cleanup skills."

"What do you recommend?"

"For one, the feds want to talk to you. Secondly, you'd best not go home, and you'd better get your extended family, such as they are, the hell out of there."

"Okay to use your trailer by the lake again?"

"I was expecting it. I'll drive out that way myself to put a key under the mat. The fewer people who know where you are, the better."

Al hung up. "Change of plans." He handed the phone to Fergie. "You'd better call Maury and Bonnie. Tell them to pack up the baby, Tanner, and anything they need for an extended stay in Clayton's trailer. They should get moving that way pronto. Make sure they aren't followed, and tell Bonnie to be sure and take her pea shooter."

The pea shooter was a Smith & Wesson Chief's Special .38, not much good for anything at a distance, but Bonnie had made it work magic in the past.

Before she made the call, she opened his glove box. His Sig Sauer was there with half a box of ammo.

"That's all we have," she said. "Will it be enough?"

"Not for what we might be headed toward."

"Should we have Maury open the gun safe and bring us anything?"

"We don't have time for that."

"And you're reluctant to give him the combination because there's money in there in addition to the guns."

"There's that. He's wrestled with temptation before. I trust him, but after our twenty years of not speaking, I am still relearning what I can about him."

"What then?"

"I'm thinking."

"Well, let me know when you've thunk."

AS SOON AS THEY CROSSED into Travis County, Fergie noticed Al slowed the truck and was watching the signs of the smaller roads that intersected with the one they were on. His look was too intense for anything like a smile, but she thought he relaxed a tiny bit when he turned left onto a small two-lane road that wove into hills and woods that would have been green any other year. Everything seemed a tired yellow or brown near the road. Grass fires had been started in the county by vehicles just pulling over to idle on top of grass as dry as it had become.

He hummed to himself and turned to the right, onto a road that felt even more narrow. Five miles later, he slowed and nodded. He turned in at a cattle gate, got out to open it, and got back in the truck. He drove on through the open gate, left it that way, and headed back down a rutted one-lane drive crowded on both sides by huge stands of prickly-pear cactus.

"Is there someone back here who might be able to supply us with a gun or two?" Fergie asked.

"We'll see."

He slowed to a stop just as they came to a bend in the road. "You'd better take the gun. Oh, and fetch out that pair of handcuffs in there."

He got out of the truck on his side, she on hers, and they headed up the lane.

"Hang back when we get to that bend ahead," he said. "I'll give you a holler if it's all clear."

At the bend, he made her a signal to stay, the same sign he used for Tanner to stay. At any other time, she might have commented, but the look on his face was far too serious.

Once he was around the corner of a stand of rust-orange mountain cedar, she eased closer and peeked around. Not a surprise. A single-wide trailer sat on a concrete slab. Cement steps, with steel piping painted white for a handrail, led up to a wider porch and the door. A small red battered Toyota truck had been parked off to one side, which suggested the resident was home.

Out in these parts, coming up to a place like this bordered on foolish. Al stooped to pick up an empty oil can from the dirt. He got closer and eased up the steps. She wished now he had taken the gun. She raised his gun to cover him but doubted it would do much good from this distance, a good fifty yards from the house.

Some birds were making a hell of a racket up in a dead tree limb off to the right. Then they went silent. Fergie's nerves tightened. She leaned closer.

Al tossed the can, which clattered against the side of the trailer. He stood to one side of the door, tight against the wall.

The front door of the trailer opened, and the screen eased open about a foot. A hand started out, holding a pistol. She wanted to scream but put her left hand up over her mouth.

Al shot forward and kicked. The gun flew upward out of the hand. While it was still in the air, he grabbed the wrist and yanked. A man came flying out through the doorway, flipped once in the air, and flopped onto the dirt. Al followed closely and leaped onto the man, twisting his arm until he was behind him. "Bring me the cuffs!" he yelled.

She ran to them and held out the cuffs.

Al dragged the guy to the front steps and put one cuff on the right wrist and the other on the steel pipe railing.

Fergie got a good look for the first time. The man was in his late twenties to early thirties, scruffy, with long blond tousled hair and a blond shadow on his chin and cheeks, which was probably as good a beard as he could grow. The beard was the sort that "back in the day" was called a basketball beard: five on a side. He wore a black AC/DC T-shirt over plaid Bermuda shorts and flip-flops, though he had lost one flip or flop in his aerial path to the ground. The guy began calling out some pretty salty vocabulary while Al went over and picked up the gun from the ground and showed it to Fergie. The pistol was a chrome-plated H&R .38 with a five-inch barrel.

"I hope we can do better than this," she said.

"Meet Ford Sweetings," Al told Fergie. To Ford, he said, "You know you're not supposed to be carrying. Tsk. Tsk. Tsk."

He eased around Ford and went inside the trailer. Fergie waited outside with Al's Sig Sauer held down at her side. Ford ignored her and continued to cuss out Al, who was banging around inside, opening and shutting cabinet doors.

Al came back out the door a few minutes later, carrying a bigger pistol and a sawed-off double-barreled shotgun. The work on the shotgun looked homemade. The butt, where it was sawed, was unvarnished wood, and the shortened end of the two barrels showed silver-bright steel. Al had two boxes of ammo as well as a handheld fifty-thousand-volt Taser. What Sweeting was doing with a Taser was beyond Fergie. But probably thinking, *You never know*, Al had taken it along all the same, as well as a small zippered canvas bag with handles in which to carry the stuff.

"This is more like it." He handed the pistol to Fergie, a Ruger .357 with a six-and-a-half-inch vent-rib barrel. "Will that do for you?"

She nodded and handed him the Sig Sauer, which he tucked inside his belt at the small of his back. He took out his phone and punched in a number.

When he got an answer, he said, "Hey, Victor. Isn't Ford Sweetings on parole?"

At the response, Al said, "I thought so. You'd better send someone over to his place. He has a piece as well as the makings to start whipping up some more meth. Oh, and can I get my handcuffs back from you later? Fergie might get in the mood for something kinky."

Fergie gave him an eye roll.

Al hung up. "We'll leave the H&R here, just out of his reach. That'll put Ford here back inside for a goodish spell."

Sweeting was still yelling at them as they went back to the truck, got in, and backed out of the drive.

"We'll leave the gate open. I'm betting deputies will be wanting to come on through in just a few minutes."

"I like the way you shop," Fergie said.

"People like Ford exist to provide for the needs of others. In this case, it's not just meth to users. He had all the fixings for that inside and was just starting up to brew a batch. That should give Victor something to chew on in addition to the possession-of-a-gun-while-on-parole rap."

The truck roared up the highway. Al was humming to himself again.

"THAT SHOULD HAVE FELT better," Lee said.

"Well, we got the sonuvabitch. So that's that."

"It should have felt, you know, more satisfying." From the first moment he had learned his wife, Brenda, had been seduced by a man in a position of some power, a rage had burned inside him. Talking with Garson, who was just as angry, had only stoked the fire. When he looked into Garson's eyes, he saw the same kind of hurt, confusion, humiliation, and betrayal he himself felt. They possessed the training and skills to do something about it, and now they had.

Lee and Garson had met when their wives were giving their depositions, statements, whatever they called it. Their eyes met. They knew. And now they'd killed the man. *But will the gnawing inside stop?* He'd have to wait and see.

What he knew initially was that whatever had happened, however that wily and slick Bentley had seduced his wife, she had blamed Bentley, then she had blamed Lee for not being more sympathetic. Home life, when he was back around her, had turned nasty. None of his doing, but he knew who was the turd in the punchbowl: that damned Bentley. And from what he could tell early on, there was a good chance that sonofabitch would get off scot-free. Whatever insane idea was burning inside him was the same one he could see in Garson's eyes too.

Their anger was flames compared to that of Brandon Highwater, that backwoods hunter dude, who had at least said what they were thinking: "Someone ought to do something about or to that Bentley." He had the enthusiasm of a big puppy done wrong. But he was right. They had needed to do something.

Their lives at home had turned into living hells, and Garson's leave was about to run out. The clock had been ticking against them. Yet they had plenty of ammo for the guns they owned... and now they had done it. They were at the other end. *Why doesn't it feel a helluva lot better than this?*

"Now the only pesky chore is to get shed of those eyeball witnesses," Garson said. "We've got to do a cleanup on those two."

Lee nodded, tired and with a bitter taste in his mouth. He agreed. It had to be done. If that would only end it, Lee thought, and end it clean. But hell, they were in it now.

Chapter Eight

Maury had the doors and trunk of Fergie's car open and was just putting a box of clothes into the trunk. Bonnie came from the house to the car, carrying the baby's car seat. She glanced around with little birdlike jerks of her head, peering into the woods around the house. Since the year had been far from green, she could see farther through some open spaces than usual. She froze when she looked up the high hill on the adjacent lot that Al had bought long ago to buffer his house. "Oh, great purple pollywogs."

She rushed to the car and tossed the baby's chair into the back seat.

"That's no way to—" Maury started to say.

"Shhh." She went to the front seat and opened the glove box. *Good. It's here.* She reached in and took out Fergie's Glock.

"What are you...?"

Bonnie tugged her Chief's Special out of the back pocket of her jeans and handed it to Maury. "You get inside and stay close to the baby. Don't you let anyone near Little Al. No matter what you hear outside, you stay with the baby. Hear?"

He nodded and took off in a loping run back to the house.

She chambered a shell and started out and around through the thickest growth she could find. Everything was so dry and crackly it was like trying to walk on Rice Krispies and stay quiet. *Impossible.* She looked down before placing every step and moved as quickly as she dared, around and up the back side of the hill. Years of hunting in the woods with her daddy, who had taught her to shoot the eyebrows off a flea, had meant a lot of fresh game in the house. Now, all that training could mean a lot more.

In the past, a sniper had set up on that hill, and Al had taken care of him. But Al wasn't here. Around her, some of the mountain cedar was still green, though looking a little puny after weeks of drought. She eased around a stand, and there he was. A man stood beside the foot-wide trunk of a juvenile live oak tree. He had a rifle with a scope and had done the trick where he'd taken his belt and put it around the tree and slipped the gun through it to give the rifle a sure and steady rest, a sniper skill.

"Hey, you!" she shouted, running forward toward him. She held her pistol extended.

The man never hesitated. He spun around the tree until the rifle was pointed at her.

She squeezed off three quick rounds while on the run toward him, the gun bucking in her hand. She held the grip tight and steady, bracing herself to hear the rifle fire.

But the guy's eyes opened wider as he slumped to the ground, letting go of the butt of the rifle.

She got to him and held the barrel of her gun fixed on his face. Then she lowered the gun and bent closer. He looked to be younger than herself, maybe late twenties, early thirties. Blond scruff of a week-long beard, hair cut short, black T-shirt over jeans and boots. Blood seeped through the fingers of one hand as he stared at her.

"They told me to wait, but..." His eyes lost their focus and stared off at nothing. He was gone.

Bonnie took out her cell phone and punched in a number. When he answered, she said, "Al, you know that threat? Well, problem solved."

"What do you mean?"

"A sniper was setting up above the house. I just took him out like last week's trash."

"Good for you, but that's not quite going to do it," Al said. "There were two of them."

"The guy's dying breath was about 'they.' Do you really think there are even more than two?"

"Just get the hell out of there as fast as you can. I'll take care of calling the sheriff's department. It's getting so they just love to hear from me."

"Shouldn't I stay by the body?"

"You leave. Now! Clayton will know where to find you for a chat. You need to be gone."

AL AND FERGIE PULLED up behind Fergie's car at the trailer late in the afternoon, when the day was cooling down to only a hundred degrees or so.

Clayton had put the trailer on its lot near enough the lake to enjoy the mosquitoes and sounds of boaters and jet skiers *yee-haw*ing from one end of Lake Travis to the other.

Maury was sitting in one of several lawn chairs set up under the awning. He waved a Diet Coke at them. In his other hand, hanging down at his side, he held Bonnie's Chief Special. "I'm on guard duty. Bonnie said no beer either. We're on full alert."

"You're sure no one followed you?" Fergie asked.

"Bonnie thinks that jasper was on his lonesome. Her words. But we zigzagged all over half the county, making sure we saw no one on our tail."

Al heard tires crunch on the gravel of the drive. A small white chalky cloud rose from behind the sheriff's department cruiser coming their way.

When it stopped, Sheriff Clayton climbed out of the driver's seat. He was alone.

"Al. Al. Al. I ask you to do something as simple as looking into the report of a chupacabra, a mythical beast that probably doesn't even exist, and the next thing I know, you're stirring up World War Seven out there."

"Well, I—"

Before Al could finish, Clayton turned to Bonnie, who was just coming down the stairs. "And you, Miss Annie Oakley, do you ever think to just clip one of these people you aim at instead of sending them to their reward?"

"He was pointing a rifle at me. I'm sure if Al was there, he would have sneaked up and knocked the tattoos off the guy so you could have an enlightening chat with him. By the way, keep it kind of down out here because I have a sleeping baby inside who just got settled."

The sky was growing darker. Al slapped at a mosquito outlined by the patina of sweat on his forearm. A tiny rivulet of sweat headed down Fergie's temple. One thing he liked about her was that she was no complainer. She stayed fixed on Clayton, who eased into one of the chairs and accepted the Diet Coke Bonnie held out to him.

"This Cynthia Standerblum you mentioned in your statement about the little kerfuffle out at Bentley's cabin—"

Fergie let out an unladylike snort.

Clayton frowned at her. "Has proven to be as elusive to the Secret Service agents as she was to my staff, who you consulted privately on this."

"Meat Jenkins—" Fergie started to say.

Clayton held up a hand. "Let me get to this, or we're going to be out here until it's as dark as the inside of a cow."

"Hey, that's my line," Bonnie said.

"I appropriated it," Clayton said.

"Well, wear it in health then," Bonnie said.

Clayton tilted his head at her for a second before turning back to Al.

"Anyway, it turns out she probably had little to do with the shooting itself but was just a bit of backstory that drew you out to Bentley's place for your timely intervention."

"Which we explained clearly enough in our statement," Al said.

"Humpf. Let me finish here," Clayton said. "The issues here are the men who took exception to the late senator messing around with their wives—or attempting to do so."

"But I took out at least one of them," Bonnie said.

"I wish I could tell you that you did. Unfortunately, the Secret Service boys tell me that their pet theory is that there were at least three exasperated husbands. The one you plugged and would have left for the coyotes if Victor hadn't taken a crew to work the crime scene, was a guy named Brandon Highwater. He was a hunter but didn't have the military background or chops in general of the other possible two. Highwater's wife didn't succumb to the senator's advances either, but he and she were headed for a divorce anyway, so in some twisted sense of Southern honor he must have put in with the others to do harm to Bentley, blaming him somehow. The Secret Service boys also think the remaining two know about Al now, and they are pretty good at cleanup."

"Just who are these two other jaspers?" Bonnie asked.

Clayton hesitated. "There are some ideas—theories really, at this stage—and I'm going to let Al fill you in on the wispy bits of that. Let's just say that the possibility stirred me enough to have you all hole up here at my place. If you've had a chance to check the media, and I suspect you may have been too busy for that, you'd know this is an extremely high-profile case. I'm hoping it's wrapped up quickly before any of you have reason to worry."

"Well, we didn't ask to be part of it," Fergie said.

"I know." Clayton nodded. "Wrong place at the wrong time."

"You sure you have even a vague hunch about who the guys were who put egg on the faces of those Secret Service men guarding a senator?" Bonnie asked.

"What I have comes from the feds, and it's just a very high probability. Hell, Al was right there, and he can't even tell us much. So if you happen to talk to anyone in the media—and heaven help us if you do—don't speculate, and use the word 'alleged' a lot. *Capisce?*" Clayton stayed fixed on Bonnie. "For the moment, I'm going to need a statement from you to take back to the office with me and share with those voracious and ticked-off feds. Al, you and Fergie may want to help her draft it. You know the sort of intel we need."

Bonnie sighed. She stood and started up the stairs. "I do believe we're getting more good out of your hideaway place than you are."

"I won't argue with you about that," Clayton said, "but my day will come."

Bonnie stopped and looked back at the sheriff. "Just one question. If the feds think they have even a rough idea of who these guys are, then Al and Fergie just maybe seeing their faces doesn't matter a whole heck of a lot, does it?"

"You can't just 'think' such things. You have to confirm them. Prove them in court. For all the shooters at the cabin know, Al and Fergie are eyeball witnesses who could be used to testify against them. Plus, they might just be ticked off now since someone knocked off one of the ones who was helping them."

"Oh." Bonnie scurried the rest of the way up the stairs and into the trailer.

Chapter Nine

Fergie came out of the bathroom dressed in jeans, a white blouse, and red cowgirl boots just as Al came in the motel room's door, carrying a couple of to-go cups of coffee he'd purchased from the adjacent gas-station convenience store.

"We're living large now." Fergie reached for one of the coffees. "But it did give us a reason to shop for some new clothes since we didn't dare visit your place for any of our stuff."

"And it gave me a chance to stock up on those little bottles of shampoo with built-in conditioner." Al took a sip from his cup and managed not to shudder. *Maybe we'll spot a McDonald's. We could get a better coffee there.* They were too far out into Bumfart Nowhere, Texas, to hope for a Starbucks. "Victor let me know that a county cruiser is going by my place every now and again, keeping an eye out. But they have little hope of spotting a couple of crack veterans like we're dealing with."

They gathered up their small tote bags, both new, and headed out to the truck. The sun was barely up, but it was a blister of a day that seemed headed toward becoming seriously warm. Al glanced around at what there was of the town: the motel, gas station, and half a dozen houses, two of them claiming to be antiques shops by day to the passing motorists who zipped through the town on their way to somewhere else. The town's name was Hi, but it should've been called Bye. One of those "blink and you've missed it" places along the road. They were near enough Armadillo Springs they probably would be there in under an hour.

"Are you pretty sure about coming all the way out here to see this fellow?" Fergie asked. "The odds seem long that he might just happen to know this Cynthia gal."

"I'm only giving the hunch any strength at all based on Mo. He hinted that there's a close community of those in the fraud-and-scam business, that many of them know each other, and that our guy here, Harley Ray Luther, sometimes puts some of them up when they're on the run."

"You trust Mo?"

"Not at all. But I doubt very much he ever does anything without a reason, and that reason is what's tugging me this direction."

"Even if it's a trap?"

Al would have shrugged if he wasn't driving. "The thing about folks like these, scammers and such, is that they're very rarely violent or threatening. It's all about guile with them, being trickier than the average person they meet."

"Well, I just hope they aren't trickier than us," Fergie said.

They passed wide-open ranches of cattle and the occasional horse ranch. They even spotted a few goat farms as they neared their destination. A tannery stood on the outskirts of the town, which according to a sign they passed, claimed over three thousand residents. A small park on the left had a swing set, a circular walkway, and a watermill beside a creek that had no water and was showing off its bed of pale roundish rocks.

The town itself was a couple of blocks long. Many of the stores had the false fronts of the western towns of the past. Al saw a hardware store, a feed store, a diner, and the usual assortment of corner gas stations, drive-thru fast-food shops, and one or two tiny churches. He slowed when he saw a grocery store and pulled into an angled parking spot in front of it.

"A small grocery in a town like this is like a post office," Al said. "With no big-box grocery chain store in town, this is it. You have to shop here. Everyone knows everyone."

They went inside, and a bell hanging from a ribbon on the inside of the door jangled. A window air conditioner high on one wall was struggling to keep the room at least tepid. A musty smell of stale crackers and dust rose up from the wooden floorboards, which looked swept but didn't look particularly clean.

"Be right with you. Feel free to browse about," called out a man in the back.

Behind a counter housing an old-fashioned cash register, he was wearing a white shop apron and speaking to a grizzled old fellow who looked like a Death Valley Scotty sort to Al. That man's frizzy grey hair and beard looked uncombed, with a curl more from dirt and sleep than from any plan. He wore what looked like a khaki hunting jacket with many pockets that hung loosely from him.

The front of the store had two halves. This side went back to the cash register. An open doorway in the wall led to another section of the store. All Al could see in this side were canned goods, many of them beans, as well as whole skids of soft drinks and racks and racks of chips. If he didn't want Pepsi or Ruffles, he had to go through the door.

Even after bracing himself, Al was rocked back on his heels once he passed through to the other side. He stopped in his tracks, and Fergie bumped into him.

"What...?" she started to say then stopped herself once she was around him and could see what he was seeing. "Oh my stars."

"This is the fresh produce portion of the store?" Al looked around. *Yep.* He couldn't see any more to the room. *This is it.*

A slanted waist-high wooden bench ran across a portion of the far wall. On it lay three heads of iceberg lettuce turning yellow and a couple bundles of carrots, the greens of which were ahead of the lettuce and had made it to brown. Two heads of celery were close enough to the edge that they drooped in the middle, and half of each head hung over the side like something from a Salvador Dali painting. None of the vegetables were wrapped. They all looked tired and unhappy.

On the other side of this room, more stacks of unrefrigerated canned soda and beer were surrounded by more racks of corn chips, tortilla chips, and pork rinds.

Al leaned closer to Fergie and whispered, "I don't think of myself as an out-and-out foodie, but I do like fresh and different. I think I'd have to kill myself if I lived here. Nope. I don't know that I could live in a town like this."

She just nodded, unable to speak.

They headed back into the main room of the grocery. The weathered fellow was just getting to the Vietnam War, a story the clerk, who had "Max" embroidered on his apron, had apparently heard more than once. Perhaps many more times than once. He turned his head enough to see them. The grizzled talker shifted to give them his full attention. Fresh meat. New listeners. The store clerk looked relieved.

The sound of the man's voice changed, taking on a deeper narrative resonance, a storyteller's tone. He'd shared this tale enough times to give it a rehearsed quality.

"It was up on Hamburger Hill that they pinned us down." He went on for fifteen minutes, sharing plenty of detail, especially about his wounds and being carried out of there.

Al had military experience in his background, and he'd heard many a similar story. He let the man talk. It wouldn't hurt much, and maybe it was a small way of saying thanks that his own wounds had been nothing as serious.

Finally, the guy wore down. He didn't look embarrassed that he'd gone on so but more like he'd just thought it might be a good idea to take a nap. He slumped toward the door. He glanced back, and when Max turned to put something away on a shelf, the guy slipped a can of tuna into one pocket and a can of beans into the other.

He went out the door.

"Did you know that man took a couple of things?" Fergie said.

Max nodded up to where the walls met the ceiling. "I know." Long mirrors instead of crown molding ran along each side, where he could see everything that went on in the store. "I just add little things like that to the bill for the Charles P Ranch. Quite a few of them are a little that way. I own this place, by the way."

The sign outside said Coy's Grocery, so that made him Max Coy.

"That garrulous fellow you just met is One-tooth Charlie," Max said.

"But he has all his teeth," Fergie said.

"They just say that because all he needs to do is get one tooth in you, and he'll have you and your wallet skinned like a mink."

"So you folks from town have an idea of what goes on at that ranch?" Al asked.

"If we have ideas, we keep them to ourselves. Those folks that come and go amount to a serious chunk of this town's revenue. We don't exactly cater to the tourist trade here. Now, what can I get for you folks?"

"Might as well pick up a few things," Fergie said.

Al picked out the kind of food he usually got for road trips or stakeouts: beef jerky, Diet Cokes, and those little packets of cheese-cracker sandwiches with peanut butter inside. Just the sort of thing this store featured. Fergie managed to find a box of breakfast bars that claimed to be healthy, as well as a couple of small containers of orange juice, once she'd checked their sell-by dates carefully.

As Al paid the bill, he asked, "Did you ever meet the guy that runs the Charles P Ranch?"

"Yep. We've met."

Max had gone taciturn on Al as quickly as that.

"Is it a fellow named Harley Ray Luther?"

"You can ask him yourself. That's him yonder." Max nodded toward the front door.

One-tooth Charlie was standing outside next to a younger man with dark hair slicked back and the face of a weasel. He seemed to be trying to dress like the late Steve Jobs.

"I never did understand those black turtlenecks," Fergie said.

The man spun and walked away, One-tooth Charlie tagging along.

"I guess he has business elsewhere first." Max shrugged and slid Al's paper bag across the counter to him.

"But you kind of know what he does, right?" Al asked.

"Yep. I'm a church elder on top of it. But dern if this town could do without his trade. He'll be back. He's one of the best customers I have."

"I can see why, nice place like this and all." Al took Fergie's hand, and they headed for the door.

"Why, thanks," Max said.

Al eased Fergie outside before she could say anything.

"Well, we've been made," she said as soon as they were on the sidewalk.

"I suppose so." Al looked up and down the street but didn't see who he was looking for. "That Charles P Ranch? Do you suppose that's a hat tip to Charles Ponzi, someone who might just be this guy's patron saint?"

"Oh, this guy's nothing like a saint," Fergie said. "Where to now?"

"I'm not sure. Hanging around here probably isn't going to do us much good. But at least we have grub for the road."

"I'll go along with grub all right."

LEE SCRAMBLED AWAY just as the two FBI agents were coming out of the diner. He ducked low behind a row of cars and slid into the driver's seat of a Corolla they'd rented with cash from a cheapo rent-a-wreck sort of outfit near the airport.

He checked the GPS-tracker app on his phone.

"You got a read on them?" Garson asked.

"Yep. 'Now the who-watcher is watching you,' as a kid's magazine I read once while waiting in the dentist's office used to say."

"It'll at least give us a chance to think creatively if we get an opportunity."

"I'll bet your wife never gave you credit for being creative," Lee said.

"Let's not talk about my wife just now, okay?"

Chapter Ten

"What are you thinking about so deeply?" Fergie asked him. They had just crossed back over into Travis County, and Al was feeling a little of the tug of the horse smelling its barn and eager to be home. "I'm mulling over a Plan B. But I don't care for it very much."

"Why?"

"It may give Maury a break from being in a trailer with a crying baby. But it could mean you and I are back to sleeping in bunk beds in that same trailer."

"At least we'll have Tanner with us."

Al was watching a black dot in his rearview mirror grow bigger until he could see a black SUV with tinted windows and government plates moving toward them at a very fast pace. "Well, crap on a biscuit."

He was plodding along at the speed limit in the right lane. The black SUV pulled into the fast lane and eased up beside him. The window on this side rolled down, and the man inside, wearing a white shirt and tie, pointed for Al to pull over.

"I think these gents want something," Fergie said.

"I'll just bet they do," Al said. "And they're probably not selling tickets to the Policemen's Ball, or Special Agents' Ball in their case."

Once he'd pulled over, the man who'd been in the passenger seat got out and walked to the driver's-side window while tugging on a dark Armani-looking suit jacket despite the heat. He did so to cover the De-Santis holster Al could see briefly, probably housing a Glock 22 with Bu-standard .40-caliber ammo. Maybe the suit was a Hickey Freeman.

At least that's what special agents wore back in the day when Al was first doing detective work for the sheriff's department.

The guy waved for them to come get inside the SUV's back seat. He patted Al down, but Fergie shook her head and shot around past him and slid inside before he could lay hands on her. He frowned but got into the front seat, shut his door, and turned to them.

"I'm Perkins. He's Scholling." The driver turned in his seat to look back at them.

"Kind of unusual to see your sort doing traffic duty. But I was at or under the speed limit," Al said.

"Knock it off," Scholling said.

They both had fairly dark short hair in the sort of faux Mohawk cut Al hadn't grown to like. Their blockish, clean-shaved faces had the stern look that gets painted into place at Quantico.

"You know why we're here," he continued.

"Actually, we don't, or even how you managed to track us down," Fergie said.

"You want to stay off the grid, don't use credit cards, and switch out your vehicle for something different. If all people were as easy to find as you were, they wouldn't have sent us in. We're sort of the Hawkeye and Trapper of our line of work in the Bu," Perkins said.

"Well, shouldn't you be out looking around for your two suspects instead of slowing us from our appointed rounds?" Al said.

"Don't be a smart-ass," Scholling said.

"He does it with almost no effort at all," Fergie said.

The two in the front glanced at each other then turned back with even sterner looks.

"Do you have any idea how big this is?" Perkins said. "There's an enormous public stink, with a senator dead and all."

"There'll be more senators. They practically grow on trees these days," Al said.

"Or in sewers," Fergie said. "This senator was stinking a bit before someone plugged him."

"You don't know how big this is," Scholling repeated.

"Not to me," Al said. "I'm just the department's chupacabra man, and retired at that."

"You don't care that someone gunned down a US senator?" Perkins asked.

"It didn't happen while I was watching him," Al said.

"And some think he was no prize in the first place," Fergie said.

Perkins came close to giving her a sneer. "Are you just upset because he didn't come on to you?"

"Oh, he came on, all right. He couldn't help himself. Just because his constituents were stupid enough or ill-informed enough to elect him doesn't sanction or forgive any of his actions. You are starting to make me think those two killers you can't find had a good idea."

"Don't forget that their current good idea is probably to take you two out." Scholling's serious face came close to winking at Perkins.

"Then you should be out finding them if you're able." Al was struggling not to just frog each of these two in the nose a good one.

"Don't you worry about that," Perkins said. "When it comes to the chase, including tech hunting, we make your Meat Jenkins look like a Cub Scout beginner."

"At least those two we're after were smart enough to use cash and keep moving about. But we'll find them," Scholling said. "The two of us have the best record for doing that in the Bureau."

"Well, let us leave you to your pursuit." Al opened his door and got out.

Neither of them called out for him to stop.

On the way back to his truck, Al leaned close to Fergie and muttered, "Having exhausted any digital means of finding those two, I'm afraid they'll have to revert to classic hunting techniques."

"Ah." She nodded. "You think they'll plan on using us as bait?"

"Without hesitation."

AL HAD GONE ONLY A mile before he slowed down, letting the brown Kia Soul behind him go out around him in the fast lane. He ignored the frown of the driver as he went past.

"What's the matter?"

"I'm trying to think like these guys."

"Which guys? The Special Op and the SEAL?"

"Yeah. If, in fact, they were the shooters. Those Bureau guys think they're pretty clever, but if I was someone who wanted to put us in the crosshairs, I'd just follow the FBI and let them lead the way to us."

"You think that's possible, even probable?"

"Oh yeah." He turned onto the next exit, which led down to an intersection with a smaller road that led up into a winding hilly road. "If I were the shooters looking for a lead to us, I might just look around for one of these black SUVs driving around, get on its tail, and follow it right to us."

While he was easing into the turn to the right, he glanced left. A huge white dump truck with a piled-high load of rocks bounced clumsily down a ramp on the far side, veered across the lanes and, with its engine roaring loudly, surged right in front of Al's truck.

Al stamped hard on his brake and slid to within inches of the side of the truck. He could see the driver inside, turning a glare toward Al. The man driving wore a black ski mask this time, but the camo outfit was the same.

Al shifted into reverse, backed up as quickly as he could, and peeled out in the other direction, just missing a car crossing a lane to head up a ramp.

The dump truck turned behind him, getting ready to follow. This way was even hillier. *So be it.* He glanced to see if Fergie had her seat belt on. She was also reaching up to grab the handle above the door so that she could hang on through any sharp turns.

Fergie's lips were pressed tightly together. Al turned back to focus on the road ahead, already starting to snake left and right up a hill in sharp turns.

The truck filled with rock should have a hard time of it but was gaining. Al could hear the roar of its engine as it strained while the driver forced every bit of power out of it.

Al had hoped to pull away, but going down the hill on the other side, the truck was gaining on them, with all its weight. At any second, it could smash into the back of them. Al pressed even harder on the gas and shot away.

"It's time," he said.

"I'm with you." Fergie reached beneath her seat and took out the canvas bag of weapons they'd taken from Sweeting. She unzipped it and pulled out the sawed-off shotgun.

"I'd go with the Ruger. The shotgun will just spray pepper at this range. No stopping power unless we had deer slugs."

Fergie switched out, trading the sawed-off for the pistol, and rolled down her window.

No one was coming from the other direction, so Al eased his truck into the left lane so Fergie could get a bead on the truck.

She undid her seat belt and leaned out her window, looking back. *Bam! Bam!*

Al watched two tennis-ball-sized holes appear in the passenger side of the dump truck's windshield.

They started up another hill, and Al pressed for all the power he could get to gain a little distance. The dump truck's weight was holding it back, and the gap widened. Its engine roared, and black smoke poured in a rushing plume from the exhaust pipe sticking up beside the cab.

A dump truck was a hell of a vehicle to use in a chase, but its driver didn't seem to mind. He squeezed more speed out of the big lumbering thing than Al had expected.

They started down the other side of the hill in tighter switchbacks meant to slow them. But the truck hugged the insides of the curves and skidded through them, gaining on them again.

Fergie was looking back for another opportunity to shoot. "I'll go for the tires this time."

"You'd better buckle up," Al said, "the low-end curve here is a pip."

She strapped herself in but held onto the pistol.

At the bottom of the hill, Al was going way faster than he should have or felt comfortable with. He let up on the gas as he hit the curve at the bottom and, at the peak of the bend, hit the accelerator to push him through the turn. His truck slid a bit and fishtailed but made it. He started up the next upward slope.

Behind him, the truck powered into the turn, screeched as the driver braked, then tipped up on two wheels. The dump truck wobbled for a moment, then the load of rocks it was carrying got the best of it, and it fell over on its side and tumbled sideways down the hill a couple of times.

Al hit the brakes. Nobody was coming. Nor did anyone follow. They'd had the road to themselves. He swung his truck around and went down to where the dump truck had gone off the road.

They got out and went to stand on the shoulder of the road, looking down.

Way down at the bottom, a good two hundred yards away, the truck lay smoking on its side, leaning against the boles of two large trees. Steam rose from its crumpled hood.

"Well, that's that." Al reached to wipe sweat from his forehead.

"Not just yet," Fergie said.

A man, still wearing his ski mask, was clambering out of the truck's cab, limping.

"Well, crap on a biscuit," Al said.

The man lifted a hand, and Al heard a shot. He and Fergie ducked. They were far enough away that a pistol was far from effective, but someone as skilled as this man might make it work or just get lucky.

Fergie lifted her pistol and squeezed off two rounds that slammed into the side of the truck with banging clangs that sent the man diving for cover.

They ran to the truck, and Al had it moving while Fergie was still closing her door.

Neither said a word until they'd gone at least ten miles.

"I don't know that I'm going to get used to this, living on the run with danger popping up far too often," Fergie said.

"Oh, I don't know. You might get a taste for it after a spell."

At the first chance, he turned off until he was headed in the direction he knew he needed to go. He checked the gas gauge and looked all around. Barring any more unscripted surprises, the rest of their trip shouldn't take them too much longer.

GARSON CAME LIMPING up the hill to where Lee had pulled over. He reached to swing open the passenger door of the Prius he'd liberated from a mall parking lot. He could hear sirens approaching in the distance. "Are you okay?"

"No, I'm not okay." Garson yanked off the ski mask and tossed it into the back seat.

"Are you hurt bad?" Lee started to pull away as Garson was still slamming his door shut.

"Now I'm supposed to say, 'Is there such a thing as being hurt good?'"

Lee frowned. "What do we need to fix you up?"

"Let's swing into a drug store once we're the hell and gone from here."

"I thought that would have gone easier," Lee said.

"It would have if that son of a beanbag hadn't swerved all over the place. And I gotta tell you, a dump truck is no vehicle to have to drive in a chase."

"Well, you did pretty well, except for wrecking the truck and damn near killing yourself."

"Don't patronize me. If one of my legs wasn't so sore, I'd kick you all the way back to the Middle East."

"Well, they sure enough don't want me back there." Lee chuckled. "Those are some of the only people on earth who want me less than my wife."

Chapter Eleven

"Where are we going now?" Fergie asked. "And are we nearly there yet?"

"Those agents were right about one thing. We've got to remove our blip from the screen—their screen and that of those two who took out Bentley and now may see us as witness threats."

"What do you have in mind?"

"We've got to pretty much avoid going to my bank or going to Meat Jenkins either to get some untraceable burner phones. And we need cash if we're going to be able to switch out the vehicle."

"Narrows it down a bit." Fergie opened one of her breakfast bars and took a bite. "We could rob a guy like Sweeting."

"Nope. Victor texted me that there was over fifty thousand in cash in the trailer. I saw it, didn't touch it. That's not the kind of money I want to be spending."

"I admire your scruples." Fergie put a container of orange juice in her beverage holder. "What else is there?"

"I was hoping not to have to resort to this, but off we go."

He drove past the goat farm where Flora-Ida and her chupacabra resided and on through Marble Falls, a town that had no falls and had granite instead of marble. Ah, the whimsy of the pioneer naming system.

He drove up 281 North and turned off at Park Road 4.

"It's a shame we're too late in the season and in the middle of a drought." He waved at all the brown and drooping plants around them. "This is one of the great spring roads to drive through to see wildflowers of every kind: bluebonnets, Indian paintbrush, and later brown-eyed Susans, along with Mexican hats."

Fergie didn't beef about the commentary. She enjoyed the long drives through the winding Hill Country roads in the spring as much as he did.

A sign said Inks Lake wasn't too much farther ahead, but Al drove up a hill and turned in to a roadside rest. No longer the full-service kind with restrooms, these had become picnic areas at best. This one had a green metal picnic table bolted to cement blocks in the ground. Around it, a large pile of pink granite boulders formed a peak to the hill, which looked out over the lake in one direction.

Al looked around for any new historical plaques that might have been erected. Texans loved their historical markers. One at the bottom of Mount Bonnell spoke of Big Foot Wallace taking refuge there while getting over the "flux." It had also mentioned his fiancée had eloped with someone else while he was away. Al had always suspected that might have been okay with Big Foot, perhaps part of his plan. The one at the bottom of Packsaddle Mountain—a two-humped hill, really—commemorated the last Indian battle in the area, in 1873. No new marker had been erected here.

Once they were out of the car, Fergie turned to look in the other direction and gasped. "Is that what I think I'm seeing?"

"Yep. It's a castle," Al said.

Four round stone turrets rose up on each corner and went on up to form round peaks. The castle's three-story walls were stone. All the windows were the arched kind more often seen in churches.

"That's Falkenstein Castle. Back in 1995, a Texas developer named Terry Young and his wife, Kim, visited Neuschwanstein Castle in Bavaria and loved it. They found out King Ludwig had also planned to build another castle called Falkenstein, but it was never finished. On the trip home, Terry promised to spend ten years to build a version of that castle in Texas for his wife."

"And he probably treated her like a princess." Fergie sighed.

"So I'm told. It's used for wedding receptions and stuff these days. Still has its romantic juice," Al said.

"Is that where we're going?" Fergie asked.

"Nope. We're already where we're going." Al walked up a path that led around to the back of the pile of pink granite rocks.

Fergie stayed close and watched as he came to a roundish pink boulder off to the side that stood knee high and looked like it had served as a seat for people to relax on and examine the panoramic view in all directions.

Al bent low and pushed at the rock. At first, it didn't budge. Then, after a few more pushes, it budged a little. He kept at it, getting it to tilt, pushing harder as it rocked back and forth. At last it gave, teetered for a bit, then fell over on its side.

He got onto his knees and dug with his hand. Half a foot down, he came to the top of a small metal box. He lifted it up for her to see. "Now we've been to the bank."

"How much is in there?"

"Only five thousand, but it'll serve for what we need at the moment."

"Do you have more emergency stashes like this?"

"I wish I could say yes. I was hoping not to need to dip into this one."

"Then I guess we're really up against it this time."

He nodded as he rolled the rock back into place with a soft thud.

They got back in the truck and drove away. Fergie waited a few miles before she asked, "What made you think to bury that kind of money out in the middle of nowhere?"

"For an event just like this, where we don't have any other smart choices."

"What if you had died or something and never gotten a chance to come back to it?"

"Then I guess it would have stayed there for a long time unless someone came across it, which wasn't likely."

She stayed quiet for the next several miles after that.

Al glanced toward Fergie once or twice. These quiet times let him reflect on how he had expected, even hoped, to live out his days alone. She was changing that, chipping away at it. He felt himself softening to it, embracing it, even though for someone who lived a life as violent as his could sometimes get, it made him vulnerable. He wasn't entirely sure how he felt about that, but he was glad to have her along at the moment.

AL PULLED OUT OF THE Walmart parking lot. "How easy was that? We have four burner phones now. Plus, we each picked up a spare pair of jeans."

"Not to mention you reloading your beef-jerky supply while I got some healthyish breakfast bars fit to keep me going," Fergie said. "How did you know which phones would be best for this?"

"Since we could hardly use an app from our phones to look it up, I just went by what kind we usually take off the up-and-coming perps who are running one kind of jive drug biz or another."

"I know sometimes you think you're sounding hip and cool, but you're not."

"Fer sizzle, my jizzle," Al said. "Nor will I be seventeen again. I can live with that."

"Where are we headed now?"

"To my mechanic's shop. She usually keeps two or three loaners around. They're not anything we'd want to run in the NASCAR circuit, but they'll move through the streets without leaving any digital wake. Can you punch in Maury's number on my new pretend smart-ass phone?"

It took a while for Maury to answer. At last his voice came on with a wavering "Hello?"

"Maury, it's Al."

"Really?"

"I know it's a different number. I'll explain later. I want you to meet us where Melissa works as soon as you can get there."

"Do you mean—"

"Don't say it. Just go there."

Al hung up and handed the phone back to Fergie. "We've got four phones here. Maybe you can get them to show an A, F, B, and M so when I pass them out, we'll know who's calling."

She kept her head down, busy with that, until he pulled into Dave's Automotive.

Melissa stood in the doorway and gave him a wave. She ran the mechanic's shop since her husband had climbed into a bottle some years back and had taken his hobby to its inevitable extreme. She'd proven quite competent at running the shop, keeping enough mechanics on hand, and calling for the parts needed. Al was interested in the two or three loaner vehicles she usually kept out back.

She was a medium-tall thin woman with a touch of grey in her long straight hair. She seemed surprised she had to look up at Fergie. Though Fergie was older, she had red hair. Melissa said nothing about that. Women know about these things, Al figured, and when not to mention them.

She led them out back to where two cars, a small pickup, and an SUV with almost three hundred thousand miles on it sat.

"I wouldn't trust the SUV. We have some work to do on it first. When we're done, it'll run like it barely has a hundred thousand miles on it."

Maury pulled into the shop's parking lot a half hour later in Fergie's car.

"Good." Fergie headed over to it to get her Glock out of the glove box.

"Maury, where the hell's my pistol?"

"The sheriff's department still has it. They said you'll get it back. But Bonnie used it to... you know."

"Well, dammit."

Al had moved their bags to a dark-blue Honda Civic. The bags were heavier since one of them contained the guns and ammo Sweeting had donated to their cause. At least they had Al's Sig Sauer, the Ruger, and that sawed-off that was of little use from more than twenty feet away. He thought about picking up some deer slugs.

"Which car do I get?" Maury looked over the vehicles beside the Civic. Al's truck was parked at the end of the row now.

"I thought about a cheap rental, but I want you to look a little more up against it than that. So maybe it would be best if you arrive in a cheap taxi instead."

"That's the sort of thing someone like Toby Scranston would use," Fergie said. "While we were waiting for you, I went over to the UPS store and knocked up some flimsy ID for you. There will be some clumsy backup for it on the internet if anyone searches. I put it there myself. We could have gotten some first-rate digital presence for you if Meat Jenkins did the work."

"But that would look too professional," Al said, "and we're kind of keeping our distance from Meat and anyone else who we know until the threat of these two killers who are loose lets up."

Maury nodded slowly.

Al held out a small stack of money in fifties and twenties. "A thousand dollars. Keep it hidden and pretend to be broke. That should come easy enough."

"Here's your burner phone too. Don't use your own for any reason. In fact, leave it in the glove box of my car. Leave the keys with Melissa,"

Fergie said. "We'll get a phone to Bonnie too, maybe through Clayton. We'll figure out something. Until then, don't call her for any reason."

"But—"

"I mean it. For any reason," Fergie said. "We'll straighten it all out later. Right now, it's dangerous to you and to her to communicate. We're up against some very sophisticated and dangerous people here."

"You've gone to some bother here to put me at risk," Maury said. "I am at risk, aren't I?"

"A little. But if you stick to the silver-tongue techniques that got you more ass than a toilet seat…" Al turned to Fergie. "His words, not mine." He turned back to Maury. "Then you'll be fine. Stay loose, stay casual, stay glib. You'll fit right in. I doubt if you'll need to stay more than a day or two, and you'll know one way or the other."

"Is there a real chance this will lead us to Cynthia?" Maury asked.

"It's a thin straw," Al admitted, "all we have at the moment. If I were asked to bet on it, I'd lay odds against. But, like I said, it's all we have unless you by chance turn up something out there that leads elsewhere."

Maury didn't say anything, a rare first for him.

"We checked everything we could and dug deeper than most," Al said. "By *we* I mean me, Fergie, Meat Jenkins, and a few friends at the department. And we found stuff going on, scams and frauds all over the place. You can't believe how much of the donated money and goods intended to help victims of Hurricane Harvey ended up elsewhere. But we didn't find a trace of your Cynthia. Maybe it's too soon for her to set up elsewhere in Texas if she is indeed a Texas-rooted gal as Bentley said. Or maybe she's in the wind and in some faraway spot where we'll never find her. For now, this is all we have, and it is slender and fragile. You may find nothing. But it'll get you out of the house for a spell."

"Okay." Maury nodded. "If you think our chances are as ripping good as you say, I'll do it."

Al and Fergie glanced at each other. They would need to keep digging while Maury followed this slim thread—a lot of digging and moving around.

"WE SHOULD HAVE HELD onto that Quinn guy when we knew where he was." E. J. Scholling clenched the SUV's steering wheel more tightly.

"Yeah. He's sure disappeared like that roadrunner in the cartoons. Not a blip on any of their phones and no sign of his truck. We probably shouldn't have said a thing to him, just let him run around like a chicken with its head cut off. But we had to open our mouths." Jim Perkins glanced toward E. J.

"Dammit. Dammit. Dammit."

"Our shooters aren't going to show up if they can't find him either."

"All we can do is keep driving around with our eyes open."

"And our minds blank," Jim said, glaring at E. J. now.

"Cut me some slack, okay? We've untangled worse messes than this." But inside, E. J. was far less confident than he was trying to sound. All they needed was something, some pinprick of movement that let them get back on the trail. It didn't help with Jim going all twitchy and impatient. That never helped.

Chapter Twelve

The cabbie dropped Maury off at the front gate of the Charles P Ranch. Maury had sat in silence for most of the trip while the driver shared hours of detail about growing up in Iraq and the hearty happy home life in Fallujah, how near the end, no one trusted banks, so the money was kept in vehicles that moved around constantly. Then he'd come to America, where everything was a dream. Gripping as all of that was, Maury was glad to climb out of the cab. A thin wooden arch proclaiming Charles P Ranch over the entrance at the road was the only indication they were at the right place.

Maury waved to the cabbie, who pulled away. The cab was soon a fading dot.

The ranch house was quite a ways back from the gateway. Maury began the long walk, which gave him far more time to think than he liked. He'd never been undercover before, although he'd been in some pretty dicey situations with Al, Fergie, and Bonnie. This was his first time alone, and he didn't care for it at all.

As he got closer, he could see an occasional bit of activity. Most of the classes and such, whatever they would be, would probably be done inside with Harley Ray Luther. Maury was supposed to arrive acting barely informed, and that was going to be the easiest part to play since he had no idea what to expect.

He was twenty feet from the front door of the ranch house when two men came around the corner, pushing wheelbarrows loaded with rocks. He couldn't decide if they were doing some chore or if it was recreational with them. They looked like two professional wrestlers, with muscles sticking out every which where. Maury had never been a gym rat, and he'd never wanted to look like he was made of bulging lumps of steel. That had apparently been the desire and plan of these two.

They lowered their wheelbarrow handles and looked at him.

"Afternoon, gents. I was wondering where I could find a Mr. Luther."

"I'm Sean," the black man said. "And this"—he nodded toward the equally gigantic white man with his blank, staring expression—"is Junior."

Junior nodded. His face started to smile then stopped abruptly and shifted back to an intense frown. His small staring eyes and the narrow space between them made him look a little cross-eyed.

Maury was trying to remember Al's words about this place for scams, frauds, and cons. He'd said these guys were mostly harmless on a physical level, that Maury shouldn't worry about coming to harm. At this second, he would have liked to heartily dispute that.

"We're going to have to see inside your bindle."

"My what?"

"Your bag."

Maury shrugged and held it out. He watched as Sean went through it and held up each item: spare underwear, tiny shaving kit, and his burner phone. Sean turned on the phone and checked to see if messages had gone out or come in. He tossed it back in the bag when he found nothing. He kept out Maury's driver's license, which had his photo but showed his name as Toby Scranston.

Sean nodded to Junior, who stepped close to Maury and patted him down. Maury had never felt smaller or more fragile and frail. When Junior got to Maury's ankles, he found the money, some inside each sock. He held up each sheaf of bills then put them back. He turned back to Sean, indicating Maury was otherwise clean.

Maury was doing all he could not to break into trembling. He would have felt more comfortable between a couple of silverback great apes.

Scammers, Al had insisted and Maury kept repeating to himself, *are not prone to violent or vicious crime.* He and Fergie had checked all the law-enforcement databases to which they still had access, and as far as Harley Ray Luther went, they found a few names linked to his, all never convicted, and none of them had done anything violent.

"It's a wild long shot," Al had said. "Just get in and get out as soon as you've determined nothing leads to Cynthia."

Then why do my insides want to turn themselves inside out?

"I suppose you want to meet the man."

"It's why I'm here," Maury said.

They walked on either side of him, out around the house, heading back toward what looked like an old-time ranch bunkhouse.

Maury reminded himself with every step that he was doing this for Bonnie and for Al, who had done a lot for him. But Al was also making an effort on behalf of Bonnie, so it was a double down on that. He began to wish mightily that he could just call Bonnie so that she wouldn't worry and he could hear her voice.

At the door to the bunkhouse, Sean indicated Maury should wait. Junior stood close beside him.

Sean opened the door and yelled in, "Mista Luther, suh!"

A hollow yell came from far inside. "What is it?"

"We got us a visitor."

They waited outside in the sun for five minutes before Luther came out. Al had described him as looking somewhat like a weasel. That wasn't far off. Luther's face was long and narrow, coming to a point at his chin. He wore a pencil-thin mustache, his eyes seemed to permanently squint, and his upper front teeth fought to protrude outward from his mouth like those of a rodent. Maury had a hard time picturing this man as a charmer. Maybe that was why he had switched to teaching these days.

Luther squinted at Maury and held out a hand for the ID card. Sean gave it to him.

"Toby Scranston?" Luther looked up from the card at Maury.

"Yep."

"How did you hear about me?"

"Well, um..."

Junior reached over and gave Maury's upper arm a pinch that was definitely going to leave a bruise.

"From a cellmate."

"You were incarcerated?"

"I was thusly inconvenienced," Maury said, which got a fleeting grin out of Luther.

"Where?"

"Huntsville."

"Oh, my. That's not for petty matters. What were you in for?"

"I'd rather not say."

Luther tilted his head a half inch. "Who told you about me, then?"

"Joseph Hently."

Al had researched the name, that of a real felon. He'd died in prison eight months ago. If Luther had any way of checking, and Al had suspected he would, then he'd get a confirmation. The name Toby Scranston would hold up too if the checking was casual.

Luther fingered the driver's license, halfway fondling it. "Well, Toby Scranston, why don't you tell me something insightful about yourself?"

Con men are notoriously reluctant to share real details of their past. However, they can spin any number of fanciful lies.

Maury cleared his throat then said, "When I was a small boy, my mother always used Joy as her dishwashing detergent."

Luther glanced at the two giants. His brow furrowed.

Maury pressed on. "As a young man, I had a girlfriend who switched me over to Dawn, said it cut grease better."

Luther's frown was profound now.

"So," Maury said, "unlike some folks, I know the exact moment when Joy left my life."

Luther fought to keep his frown but broke into laughter. The two big men chuckled along with him.

Obfuscation—saying nothing but making it sound like something—is a handy tool for a scammer, and Maury had just passed the first test.

"Come along." Luther waved a hand.

Maury followed as they went inside the bunkhouse. The two big men peeled away and headed back toward where they'd left their wheelbarrows, returning to their sport or labor, whatever they'd been up to back there.

Instead of the traditional bunkhouse with rows of cots on each side, this one had been made into rows of rooms on each side of a central hallway. Luther led the way down the hall until he came to the room at the end.

He knocked and, without waiting for an answer, swung the door open. The room was small, with barely room for a steel cot on each side and a small table by the wall between them. Maury had hoped for a window but didn't get his wish. It was a box of a room, sturdy and simple.

"You've got to admit, it's a cut above Huntsville," Luther said.

A man sat on the bed to the left. His grey hair stuck out every which way, and he grinned a careful and sly smile, like a cat spotting a mouse.

"This is your roommate," Luther said. "His name is Charlie."

Luther gave Maury a little shove into the room and backed out, closing the door behind him.

Maury knew from the moment he saw the grizzled fellow that this must be the One-tooth Charlie whom Al had described to him.

Charlie's grin was still stuck in place. "Fancy a game of gin?"

"I guess so," Maury said, "as long as you understand."

"Understand what?" He handed the worn deck to Maury.

"I used to be fairly handy with the pasteboards." He cut and riffled the deck, going through the motion seven times. He had spent hours practicing, back when he had aspired to doing a magic act, time he sometimes felt he'd wasted, until now.

"I expect the spots are fairly worn off them by now." Charlie's fixed smile was oozing off his face.

Maury dealt a gin hand apiece, ten cards each since there were two of them, and turned up the top card.

Charlie took the displayed ten of hearts and discarded a three of clubs.

"Tell you what," Maury said, "why don't you pick any two cards from the middle of the deck."

"You do magic as well?"

Maury grinned enigmatically. "Sure, why not?"

Charlie shrugged and reached for the deck. From the middle, he drew out the four of spades and eight of diamonds. He showed them to Maury, who nodded.

"Now hold them in your thumb and forefingers."

"Done."

"Would you rather have two aces?"

"Okay, sure."

Maury took the top two cards off the deck and turned them over. One was the ace of diamonds, the other the ace of clubs. He picked them up and turned them over. He tapped the two cards Charlie held with them. "Now what cards would you bet me you're holding?"

"A four and an eight."

"Turn them over."

Charlie turned over the cards he held. The ace of diamonds and the ace of clubs looked up at him. "What the hell?"

"Turn them over again."

"Are these going to be the four and eight again?" Charlie turned over his cards. They were two queens, one of spades and the other of clubs. "Are you kidding me? What's in your hand now?"

Maury turned over the two cards he held, two queens, one of hearts and the other diamonds.

He set them aside, picked up the gin card Charlie had discarded, added it to his hand, and flipped over his cards. "And, by the way, gin."

Chapter Thirteen

They pulled into the parking lot of the La Grange Post Office a little after one in the afternoon, their second stop of the day. Al wasn't feeling hopeful. All they had was a PO box number, and the post office was the logical place to check.

The rectangular orange brick façade outside gave way to an interior like almost any other post office Al had ever been in once they'd climbed the steps and gone inside. A plaque proclaimed this to be the site of the first rural mail route in Texas. Al supposed that the bulletin board at one end had once held wanted posters and such. Now it held community announcements. Only one mail clerk was working behind the counter.

At least the air conditioning was top notch and working heartily away while he and Fergie stood behind a woman who spent ten minutes exploring ways to send a package that eventually cost her two dollars to send. Then she wanted to look at stamps and bought half a dozen. As she turned to leave, she remembered she had to send a registered letter, which took almost another twenty minutes.

Al gave the diminutive clerk behind the counter credit for not tearing out his remaining wisps of greying hair. Most mail clerks he knew, like taxi drivers, had developed a novocaine-like calmness that allowed them to stand there with blank expressions and endure traffic jams or tedious patrons with a countenance of which Buddha would be proud—except those mail workers who snap and go "postal," but this guy didn't look remotely close to that.

When at last the counter cleared and the clerk, whose name tag said Phil, waved them forward, they showed their badges and asked if they could see the card that showed the street address for the PO box. Neither badge was active, but Clayton had encouraged Al to keep his, and Fergie had managed to hang onto hers, although she had never told him how.

Phil held up a forefinger and went into the back room. They heard him yell.

Five minutes later, a woman who looked more like a dowager duchess than a postmaster came out and looked them over. Al was glad she didn't bother to ask to see their badges again. She did give them a hairy eyeball, probably wondering if they weren't a little long in the tooth to be doing police work. But she shrugged and dug out a file box and flipped through it until she came to the right card.

She slid it over for them to see.

Al didn't need to write it down. He had the kind of memory that had absorbed the address at first glance. He nodded, thanked her, and followed Fergie, who had already turned and started for the door.

The thing about following the kind of flickering leads they'd uncovered toward one scam or another, in hints they got from the internet, was that those leads could be fresh or could be stale. All they'd had here were some complaints about what sounded like a bogus debt scam, where individuals got contacted about some supposed debt they needed to pay at once. The savvy ones ignored the request or turned it over to some form of law enforcement. But enough people paid off to make the thing profitable, for a while. Then the wise con artist would move on before the cops moved in.

This had seemed fresh enough to attract someone like Cynthia, but as soon as they pulled up to the street address behind the PO box number, the lead turned as stale as last week's toast.

The house was a pink double-wide on a slab, with a blank front picture window with no curtains. Half a dozen rolled newspapers covered the front steps.

Al got out of the car, braved the heat that seared his forehead, and peeked in the window. The place was as empty and cleared out as his hopes and dreams. He saw no furniture or pictures on the walls. The floor was covered with a worn shag carpet of an indistinguishable color and was worn through in spots. Someone had taken plastic hobby-store flowers, tulips and geraniums in this case, and shoved them into the ground in a row along the front of the house. If the attempt was to bring cheer to the place, it had failed. The sun had faded away the yellows and reds, even the green of the stems and leaves, until they just looked pale, withered, and sad, adding to the melancholy that had a death grip on the weathered house. If this building had been the thriving home of frauds and swindlers, it had passed some time ago from that flicker of glory days. *So much for the currency of information on the internet.* He shrugged for Fergie's sake as he headed back to the car.

As he drove out from the edge of La Grange and eased back onto the highway, heading east toward Houston, he thought of the Chicken Ranch, as he always did when thinking of La Grange.

That wasn't fair to the town since the place, also known as "The Best Little Whorehouse in Texas" on Broadway, hadn't been open since 1973. But just as he thought of sausages when mention of the German-established town of Elgin came up, he thought of the Chicken Ranch for La Grange. The rumor he'd always heard was that the winning team of the annual Thanksgiving Day contest between the University of Texas and Texas A&M got taken to the whorehouse as a reward, something the NCAA might frown upon these days, even if it was true back then.

He had only to look around to see still-charred open places and the absence of trees after fires had swept through the La Grange area during another recent drought a few years back. But it was that frisky Chicken Ranch business just a couple miles east of town that niggled as he drove.

Fergie took out her pocket notebook and crossed off one more from the list. "Is this the way you used to work while detecting in the county?"

"No. You know better. And I'm betting you didn't function this way in the city. But we're up against it. We could wait for Cynthia to get pinched someday and hope for some sense of justice down that road. But we'd likely never get the cancer fund's money back."

"I'm just uncomfortable with this sort of detecting."

"It does feel like a real crap shoot, doesn't it?" he said. "But we can't just sit around and hope Maury's venture leads anywhere. That was a thin thread at best."

Out on the highway, he pressed on the gas, making up time they'd just frittered away.

Fergie glanced at the open package of beef jerky on his lap. Her lip didn't curl, but she looked away.

He wondered at times if she flexed and put up with more from him than he did from her. She always got to the bathroom first in the morning, and the smell of her perfume lingered and whatever else she used by the time he went in. But he'd always planned to live out his days alone, and enough of that remained that she was careful not to push or seem needy. *Ah, well.*

"I just hope this next stop proves to be a little more productive," she said.

"Me too," he agreed.

Chapter Fourteen

Over two hours later, he was weaving through the outskirts of Houston, glad that he didn't have to drive all the way through the town. The largest city in Texas and the fourth largest in America, Houston had traffic that always came first to Al's mind when he thought of a maddening, fast-paced drive not unlike the Daytona 500, only with other drivers waving fists and fingers.

"Did we come here just to be moving about," Fergie asked, "or did you really think this might lead to Cynthia?"

"Just another long shot, about all we have for now."

Al parked the Honda half a block away from where they could see the two local police cruisers as well as a vehicle Al recognized as being from the state attorney general's office.

"Hmm." Al frowned at what was going on around the house. "It took us too long to peel through the defensive layers and get to the actual physical address. That's all. Meat Jenkins could have done in twenty minutes what it took us almost a day to accomplish."

"But we can't reach out to Meat now, can we?"

"Let's just wait and see if one of the people they bring out of there is Cynthia."

When a cuffed older couple was brought out at last and loaded into a cruiser to be taken away, Al sighed.

The moment a man in a dark-blue suit walked outside into the day's heat, Al got out and walked over to him, Fergie tagging along close behind.

"Well, Al Quinn. Whatever brings your retired butt all the way down to Houston? Please say it has nothing to do with what I'm working on here. I sure hope you don't have your nose in this."

To Fergie, Al said, "This is Sidney Draper. He's a rising star in the attorney general's office. He and I talked after I had that case involving child porn."

Sidney glowered at them. He looked like some sort of ice-hockey player, say an enforcer, crammed into a suit and just waiting for the puck to drop so he could start doing some high sticking.

"He's also done some work in cybercrimes," Al said. "But when last I heard, he was doing special investigations, some involving all the frauds, cons, scams, and swindles going on."

Sidney's frown, if anything, grew darker.

"This is Fergie, former Austin PD detective," Al said. "I'd say she's my fearless sidekick, but she's more of an equal partner."

"Why thanks, Al."

"Again, why are you here?" Sidney said.

"The Murphys. I thought what they were doing was legal, kind of. But I got wind they might be working with new people. It's the new people who interested me."

Sidney tilted his head, seeming to mull over his options about how much he dared tell Al. "These two crossed the line. They set up a fake oil well inside a barn and painted a water sprinkling system to look like oil pipelines. They used a few stringers to reel in investors greedy enough to throw money at a scheme like the Home-Stake Production Company from so many years back. Maybe they didn't think anyone remembered."

"That was in Tulsa, right?" Al said. "And among those who lost millions were Andy Williams, Barbara Streisand, Jack Benny, and even Bob Dylan. Oh, and not to leave out New York's Senator Jacob Javits."

"Al's memory," Fergie said, "is more of a curse than a blessing."

"It's these new stringers who interested me," Al said to get the exchange back on track.

"Who'd you have in mind?"

"A woman named Cynthia Standerblum."

"Ah, Cat Stevenson, aka half a dozen other aliases."

"Really?"

"Yeah. That's what I thought too the first time I heard her alleged real name. Call her Catarina if that makes you feel better."

"Do you know where she is?"

"Not a clue. I wish I did. Some of these sort of people, like Ollie and Sylvia there, who just got hauled away, are small enough I just barely hear their skittering feet, like mice heard from afar. This Cat is a far bigger... fish, if you will."

"Could you let me know if you come across her?"

"Probably not. I'd ask the return favor, but you know..."

"I hear you. Well, nice seeing you again, Sidney."

"Just stay out of my way."

They waited until the AG's car pulled away, the show over. Al reached for the key and started the engine.

So far, before the stops at La Grange and this one, they had poked at two recently started makeshift charities claiming to be helping Hurricane Harvey victims and one senior-care center where complaints had reached a noticeable high. They'd found some shifty goings-on there but hadn't come across any hint of Cynthia.

Here they were on the outskirts of Houston with once again nothing to show for gas used and eating only road-warrior food that was starting to make Al wish for a real and proper meal.

"My hopes weren't too high on this one anyway." Al wove his way through traffic heading out of the always-congested Houston area. "This scam had been running awhile, probably while Cynthia was still bilking the hospital."

The fraud had been the usual "too good to be true" sort of thing that worked better than it should. The mark would see an ad for health supplements at only $4.95, plus shipping and handling. The customer gave his credit-card number or, even worse, his bank-account information. Next thing he knew, he was out $180 before he could stop any more money slipping away. Then he would find out the transaction was legal, that he could do nothing, and his bank or the credit-card company wouldn't disallow the charges.

Done often enough with many people at this scale, this kind of operation would pay off big, but not for those two who were just being hauled away. Greed had gotten the better of them, and they'd reached out for more, crossing that delicate legal line that had only partially protected them. Al thought it a shame that neither had been Cynthia. Even if it had been, he doubted they would get the cancer fund back in all the legal tangle that would follow. Getting the cash back was an important aspect of Al and Fergie's search, and perhaps the hardest to accomplish.

Soon, the road opened up, and they were moving more briskly in a homeward direction past fields that were brown and needing rain as badly as those near Al's home. He'd heard the Lower Colorado River Authority had cut off any water going to rice fields some daring farmers had started up in this part of Texas. "Why anyone would want to start rice farming in Texas is beyond me," he said out loud.

"What?" Fergie asked.

"Nothing." He kept an eye out for a restaurant he knew of along this route, one where they could get some real home-style Texas cooking: grits and greens, fried okra, Texas toast, and beef steaks almost too big for the dinner plate.

As they were pulling into a rustic-looking place called Antlers, she looked at him and asked, "Do you feel like we're just thrashing around, and not all that successfully?"

"Yes."

"Fine. I just wanted to hear you say it."

"IS YOUR LEG BETTER?" Lee asked.

"It's okay if I keep the ankle wrapped tight. The bruises will go away. It doesn't bother me near as much as this damned waiting. I hate waiting." Probably without knowing he did it, Garson reached down to rub at his leg.

"Really? I bet you sat in a sniper position for hours on end before this."

"Yeah. But this whole thing has put me on edge."

"Should I stop at another drug store and get you some feminine hygiene products?"

"Don't you start on me."

"Just don't get twitchy on me."

"The only thing that's going to get twitchy is my trigger finger if we get the chance to wind this up and clear out of here."

"Then it's 'Mexico, here we come.'" Lee pulled over and eased the current borrowed-without-permission pickup off the road and behind a thick stand of sumac that hadn't given up the ghost yet but had turned red and was on its way to dropping its leaves.

"Are we close?"

"At least a quarter mile away. But it's as close as I dare. Wait here while I take a look at this Quinn dude's place."

"I wish that Brandon dude was still keeping an eye on it," Garson said.

"We sure hadn't heard another peep from him," Lee said. "I was hoping he got a chance to get back with his wife and took it, until we heard about him on the radio. Bit the dust."

"We told him to be careful and just watch."

"Wouldn't listen, would he?"

"If that Quinn guy's in there, you come back for me first."

Yeah, right. With Garson still limping around like Chester on *Gunsmoke*. "Sure thing," Lee said. "I wouldn't want you to miss out on any of the fun."

Chapter Fifteen

Maury got up when he heard Charlie stirring. He sat up on his cot while Charlie wrapped a sheet around himself as a robe, covering up his yellowish T-shirt with matching jockey shorts. Barefoot, he plodded off down the hallway. He was back too soon to have showered. Maury got dressed before taking his shaving kit and heading down the hallway to the communal men's bathroom at the far end of the hallway. The women, if any were staying here, had their own bathroom somewhere, maybe in the ranch house, where everything might be a bit more upscale.

Whitewashed walls lined a large open bathroom with a row of urinals on one wall, a few toilet stalls after those, and sinks and a mirror on the other side. The shower area was an open line of three shower heads over a stretch of tiles at the back. It was like staying at the Ritz Carlton. He put his shaving kit by one sink and stacked his clothes there. Taking a white towel off a short pile of them, he took one of the fastest showers of his life. He dressed again before shaving. *Whew.* Now he felt almost half human.

On a table stretching along the short hallway leading to the front door, a coffee machine had a half-full pot. Next to it sat an open box of the kind of Danish made in quantities in factories. Maury helped himself to a Styrofoam cup and a cheap napkin and took a cup of coffee and a Danish. He headed outside.

Charlie was sitting at a worn picnic table beside a toolshed. Maury went over and sat down across from him.

"Wait here," Charlie said. "Luther will come talk with you at ten."

Maury glanced at his Timex, which showed a little after eight.

"He has other stuff going on until then." Charlie rose, tossed his empty coffee cup into a trash barrel, and ambled off toward the back of the ranch house.

Maury watched other people come and go. Several came out of the bunkhouse, looked around, and headed the same direction Charlie had taken.

After a while, Sean and Junior came jogging up to the toolshed. They both wore grey sweatshirts and sweatpants. Dark vees of sweat had formed front and back on the shirts. Neither paid him any attention. They carried a weight bench out of the toolshed and set it in an open space. Then they brought out a barbell so full of weights that it bent as they carried it. They went back in for dumbbells.

Each took turns on the bench doing presses, the other spotting. After that, they started on the dumbbells. They started with seventy-pound dumbbells for their warm-up curls and flies before progressing to heavier weights. Maury doubted he could get any of them off the ground himself.

He felt something quietly threatening about the intensity of their workout, heightened by them never looking his way.

He went back to the bunkhouse and got another cup of coffee, although it looked denser and more bitter now. He poured in some dry nondairy creamer, stirred it with a finger, and went back to his spot at the picnic table.

He sure felt like he was someplace else.

Watching all the people, some twenty or so of them, scurry to their classes or whatever, all to learn to be better scammers, had a surreal feel to it. Some people, physicists for instance, believed in dimensions other than the known world. Maury'd had enough insight into some of those dimensions to make him a believer of sorts. They were like a layer of mycelium existing underground, allowing mushrooms and other fungi to pop up now and again—present but not usually visible.

Long ago, in the raging hormonal madness of his younger chasing days, he'd been in a bar during a trip to New York City and had spotted a tall woman with an Adam's apple. He knew at once what was going on there. But curiosity tugged, and he went up to her and asked a few questions about her world, another dimension to him.

She said in a low, throaty voice, "Come on."

They hopped a cab, and she took him to a club over on the bottom of Greenwich Village. At first, he didn't understand when they walked inside. The place was mostly filled with women, some youthful and cheerleader beautiful.

His escort waved a hand. "None of these are really women. Welcome to the transgender world."

He couldn't have imagined anything like it, and being there did feel like stepping through a portal to another world. He hadn't been drawn into it, nor did he want to participate. But the curious side of him just couldn't get over another whole world out there he hadn't known existed.

A tall blond woman showing a lot of cleavage that looked real and wearing a pearl choker that hid any hint of a bump on the throat came up to him and put her hand on his forearm. He politely disengaged and moved away. He was a horny young man back then, but that was not what was compelling him to look about in a place like that. What he was experiencing was the epiphany and raw amazement that whole worlds existed around him about which he knew very little.

He was later exposed to the insides of the huge world of porn and even to human trafficking. These existed at a level of which few people were aware. The same was true, as far as he knew, in the gay world, though he had no personal experience there. His chasing days had stayed restricted to the female fauna of his species.

He supposed the same was true for Al when dealing with the world of cartels and the vicious and violent criminal world. This was Maury's first drop into a world of crime so subtle that the predators seemed kind, and the ruses they worked up almost always seemed intended to help. He found it hard to believe that this dimension existed at the same level throughout America, and it was a world in which Cynthia thrived.

This sort of musing could have gone on all day, listening to the two sweat balls who were by now grunting and flexing, admiring themselves beneath their stained sweat suits—not each other, themselves.

"Toby?"

Maury was staring off at a piece of blank pale-blue sky, not a cloud in sight. Then he remembered Toby was his name at the moment. He looked up. Luther stood there, wearing the same Steve Jobs–looking crap he'd worn the day before.

Maury sneaked a glance at his watch and saw it was ten o'clock.

Luther sat down on the other side of the table. "I checked on your story. It seems to add up, but maybe not under the name Toby."

"How long have you been Mr. Luther?"

"Touché."

Maury looked into Luther's eyes and realized they were brown with little yellow flecks. He took in the pencil mustache at close range and wondered how much of a chore it was to shave it that way every morning.

"What is it you want to do?" Luther asked.

"I have skills, but I want to get better, enough to be able to put a little something back to get by on."

"Charlie tells me you have skills. He said, 'Don't ever play cards with that dude.' Now, what most interests you?"

"Whatever is most safe, fastest, and least likely to call attention to me."

"That goes for everything we do here."

"Yet people get caught sometimes."

"They do. But it's usually their own stupid or greedy fault."

"You can teach me to be careful?"

"I can teach you a lot. Careful is something that comes from you if you're a thoughtful man."

"I'm thinking real hard right now."

"Then you're on the right path."

Maury nodded and waited.

"You understand how it works?" Luther said. "You pick a course, pay your tuition, and you get informed and a chance to work on a skill."

"What are some of the options?" Maury asked.

"We have specialists for classes about tech theft and all current scams: charities for events like Hurricane Harvey, home repair, and scamming seniors."

"I don't think I have the technical chops for something like phishing, identity theft, or some of the other fancy-footwork computer stuff."

"Understood."

"Something not too smarmy," Maury said. "Like those ambulance-chasing lawyers who leap at every opportunity to squeeze money from situations like asbestos, big-rig accidents, business-vehicle accidents, and deep-pocket companies like big pharma with that talcum powder mess."

"That's a specialized area, and you need a law degree, a real one," Luther said. "With the paths we offer, you can get around that and make much more. If you do really well out there when you're done, you can buy you one of those fancy Ivory League degrees."

"Ivy League."

"I know, Toby. I know. That was a lesson right there. Never look as smart as you are."

Chapter Sixteen

When Luther headed back toward the ranch house, Maury got up and eased around to the other side of the toolshed, where he could hear the two panting big men still working out but couldn't see them.

He took the burner phone out of his pocket then hesitated. But dammit, he had a right to check on his wife and baby. Plus, what he was doing was scary, and talking with Bonnie would help calm him. He punched in Bonnie's number.

"Yes?" her answer was tentative but hopeful.

"It's me, Maury."

"Are you okay?"

"I'm fine, but I can't talk long. How are you and Little Al?"

"Should you be calling?"

"I couldn't help it. That's a good thing, isn't it?"

"I suppose. I hope Al doesn't find out and that nothing comes of it. He said not to use this phone until he gets me one like you have."

"What can it hurt? I just wanted to hear your voice."

"What do you think so far? Any sign of Cynthia?"

"No. And what I think right now is that sometimes we're just clumsy amateurs, lucky to be alive, given our meddling around with people far sharper and more dangerous than we are."

"Have they threatened you? Are you in trouble?"

"There are a couple of really big thug-looking guys here who threaten me just by their existing. But they're not the truly worrisome ones."

"Is it really that bad?"

"Listen, I'll try to call each day. If you don't hear from me, you let Al know, okay?" He tried but failed to keep a quiver from showing in his voice.

"But Al said—"

"Daily. Okay?"

"Okay." The quiver had traveled between the phones to her now.

He broke the connection five minutes later and put the phone in his pocket. He looked around. Someone had been standing at the corner of the bunkhouse, staring at him. As soon as he looked that way, the person disappeared around the corner. Maury caught only a glimpse of curly grey hair going in many directions. *Charlie.*

THE NEXT DAY, MAURY was supposed to declare his electives, as they put it, and choose what coursework he wanted and could afford. When he woke, Charlie was already out of the room. After cleaning up, Maury got his coffee and Danish and went out to sit at the table by the toolshed.

He'd gotten no instructions about when Luther would come to discuss what Maury wanted to do. It could have been his imagination or the growing knot of stress that had begun to tickle his insides, but he felt some of those going past looked his way differently. The two hulks doing their morning fitness craziness seemed to be watching him from time to time, although they had ignored him before. *Probably just nerves.* But the time seemed to stretch thin as he sat and waited.

From where he sat, he could see any vehicle that came down the lane. He watched a June bug–green Chrysler Town & Country mini-van come up the drive toward the ranch house. Just before reaching it, the vehicle turned and went over to the parking lot, where a dozen cars and SUVs and one or two trucks were parked in casual rows.

Something niggled far back in a corner of Maury's brain as he looked at the minivan. *Familiar but not familiar.*

A white-haired woman got out of the car and walked toward the ranch house.

As she got nearer on the path, she called out, "Morning, Junior and Sean."

"Howdy, Miss S.," Sean said.

Junior nodded, the veins sticking out on his temples as he manhandled two dumbbells that would have crushed Maury had he tried to lift them.

The woman gave Maury a brief glance as she went past and kept walking. Abruptly, she stopped, turned, and started back toward the picnic table.

She sat down across from him and looked at him. "Hi. I'm Candice Styvenghaust," she said. "Are you a new arrival getting ready for classes?"

She wore the type of outfit he'd seen in rest homes. He'd spent a brief tour of duty in one as a guest before his heart attack, when Bonnie had become his nurse as he bounced back from that. The embroidered name patch confirmed her name, Candice. He found himself looking at her face, which seemed too smooth for the grey hair.

Insight hit him in a wave.

He was looking at Cynthia Standerblum. His mind whirred, trying to recall on how many occasions she had seen his face at the hospital. Not many, and a lot of people worked there. She had dealt mainly with Bonnie and with Hermina Vanderhausen, the hospital administrator.

"What's your game?" she asked.

His blood froze in his veins for a moment.

"You look a lot like you were a player in your day, hmm?"

He looked deep into her icy pale-blue eyes, trying to spot a glimmer of recognition. But if she knew who he was, she was hiding it well. *Whew!*

"Are you coming on to me?" he asked.

"That depends. Why don't you sign up for one of my classes?"

"Don't you work at a rest home?"

"Senior-care center we call them these days. And yes, I do keep a hand in. A lot of opportunity there. But I also teach, to those willing to learn." She glanced at her watch, and her eyebrows rose. "Oh, I'd better get going." She stood. "If you'll excuse me. And about the class, think about it."

She took off at a walk that belied the white hair as well.

Maury sat there at the table, his insides doing cartwheels to the left and right. *Did she know? Has she recognized me?*

Chapter Seventeen

Outside the restaurant, Al paused before he got back into the car. He glanced at the Antlers sign, the one that said he could get liver and onions done seven different ways inside, proclaiming it as a dare. He'd lived up to the challenge by trying the chicken-fried liver, new and different to him and the right kind of comfort food to have in his belly while driving in a seemingly aimless way across Texas. Fergie stood on the other side of the car, waiting while he took out his phone and punched in a familiar number.

"Hello. It's me, Al Quinn. Can you get me Victor Kahlon?" He didn't even try to talk to Sheriff Clayton this time.

Putting the call through took a while for the sheriff's department receptionist. Victor was out in the county somewhere. She had to patch Al through to a cell phone. Finally, he got an answer.

"Al, is that you?"

"As advertised."

"I've been trying to get ahold of you. Did you have your cell phone turned off?"

"Maybe. What's up?"

"You know how we were having a deputy swing by your place on the lake every now and then?"

"Yeah."

"Well, they spotted someone casing your house, sneaking right up to it. They didn't go inside. Once the guy determined no one was home, he slipped away."

"Did he look like either of the two guys who probably did Senator Bentley?"

"I don't know. I didn't see the guy myself. I hurried out there as soon as I heard from the deputy who spotted the guy. But whoever had been there was as gone as the buffalo."

"I sure wish the deputy could have found out more, although if it is one of these guys, they are very dangerous. It's probably just as well he didn't tangle with them."

"I agree, since I know what they did to Bentley's cabin and probably to Bentley. Two FBI guys have been asking after you too. As soon as they heard about someone prowling your place, they rushed out there. But they got nothing as well."

THE MOON WAS A YELLOW sliver that looked like a rocking chair. Al was crawling on his hands and knees, touching ground that felt as warm as an iron frying pan just taken off the stove. Something skittered across some dry leaves in front of him as it scurried out from the gap under a flat rock over to a larger gap in the ground at the base of a sage bush. A lizard, he hoped.

As the heat of the day rose from the hard-packed soil, Al could smell the dusty, dry desert odor the scorching sun had left behind.

A glimmer of light was coming from the curtained windows of a trailer just ahead. First, he wanted a careful look around. Staying as low as he could, he made a slow, painful circumnavigation of the trailer's perimeter—painful because he banged one knee on a rock he didn't see in time and put his left hand down on a dried agarita leaf. The hollylike points stabbed him like a small knife.

When he felt sure he was the only one around, he circled back to the extended awning and eased up the steps to the door. He was reaching with his right hand to rap on the door when he heard a sound behind him, the distinctive clicking sound a hammer makes while being pulled back on a revolver.

"Stay right where you are. Reach up and grab a couple of handfuls of stars."

"Kind of hard with that damned awning in the way," he said when he recognized Bonnie's voice. He turned slowly, letting her see who he was.

She was standing in a shooter's stance, the barrel pointed right at him. If he had been someone else, he would have had a pretty hot time of it.

"Well hell, Al. What're you doing sneaking up like that? You know I'm prone to keep an eye out, especially now." Bonnie lowered her Smith & Wesson .38 Chief's Special.

Inside, the baby began to cry.

"Out of the way." Bonnie rushed to unlock the door and charged inside.

Al followed. Tanner leaped across the room and climbed up on Al's leg to get his head petted.

Al lowered to one knee to pet Tanner properly and rub his belly when he turned over. Then the dog bounced upright again and pressed closer. Tanner's tail was wagging back and forth as fast and hard as it could go. *If there's anything happier than a dog's tail wagging, I don't know what it is.* Al rubbed Tanner harder, probably as happy as the dog was for them to see each other.

"I'm glad you're being vigilant," he said when Bonnie came out of the larger bedroom, holding Little Al, and sat down on the couch. Al hoped she wasn't going to breastfeed the baby right there.

"I've been a little on edge. What brings you out this way?"

"I came to bring you this." Al held up the burner phone he'd gotten for her. "This way, you can safely keep in touch with Maury, Fergie, and myself. Just wait for Maury to call. You won't know what he's up to over there. He could be in the middle of a meeting or something."

She nodded and looked down at the phone.

But something in her expression made Al ask, "What? You two didn't already speak by phone, did you?"

"Well, yeah. But just the once."

"Even when I told you to be careful not to?"

"He's the one who called."

"And you answered with your old cell phone?"

"Yeah."

"I hope everyone in this isn't as sophisticated as I fear they are."

"You think they can find us now?"

He wanted to say no. "Maybe."

"Maury just wanted to know how I was doing and to hear about the baby."

"The call was brief?"

"Yeah." She hesitated. "And there was one other thing."

"What?"

"He was under the impression that con men, scammers, whatever kind of people would be out there would be more crafty than physical."

"And?" Al stroked the back of Tanner's neck.

"He said there were two big thugs at the ranch."

"Maybe there have been some threats to this Luther guy."

"Perhaps, but that's not what was worrying Maury."

Al waited.

Bonnie looked up at Al. "He couldn't figure out what else they might be there for, or what they might do to him if he got caught."

MAURY WOKE AND KNEW at once something was wrong, very wrong. He glanced at the cot across the room. Not only was it empty, but all the bedding had been stripped.

"Oh, no!"

He jumped to his feet. The hard floor felt cool on his soles. He rushed to the door. Locked. Of course it would be locked.

It didn't look like he was going to get any Danish or coffee this morning.

Everything about Charlie was gone.

He looked at the floor beneath the table between the beds. Maury's bag was gone. He got up, went to the door, and tried to open it again but found it locked from the outside. They'd left him his shirt, pants, and shoes, so he dressed. His fingers trembled.

His eyes started to get desperate in their sweeping. He took in the thin grey-and-white-striped mattress, all that was left of the bedding on the cot across the room. He got down on his knees and looked under the cots. He saw only a whitish ball of dust in the far back corner under his own cot.

He thought hard. *Let's see, they have my money as well as my fake ID.* He wondered if Cynthia had recognized him after all. Charlie had been the one to see him make the call. *They have her number! They have Bonnie's number now!*

Maury started around the room, feeling everything. The walls were solid. He thumped on them. The walls sounded like they were made of closely spaced studs or thick sheets of wood. No sheetrock to break through. That was no accident. No window either. He would bet this room had been soundproofed as well.

He tested the door again, thick wood on a steel frame. He hadn't noticed that before. The cell-like shape of the room had a function, one it had finally arrived at.

Perhaps the appearance of anyone new could go either way, and this room had a purpose to its design. He looked around and wished there was something he could kick.

"WHAT ARE YOU DOING?" Jim Perkins tried to see what was going on behind them in his side-view mirror. All he could see was a silver Volvo plodding along.

"I'm slowing down. I thought that was obvious," E. J. said.

"Well, why?"

"I think someone is following us."

"Really?" Jim tried to spot them in the side mirror then the rearview mirror. "Someone is tailing a Bureau SUV? Can't be the brightest turnip in the patch."

"I give these two shooters more credit than you do. It's possible they might use us to get to those witnesses."

"But aren't we the ones trying to find the witnesses to use them to get to the shooters?"

"Yeah, call it a real bucket of ironic," E. J. said. "I've sped up, and I've slowed down, and this jasper behind me has been glued to me like he's attached by a trailer hitch."

"You really think it's—"

"I don't think anything yet." E. J.'s voice grew louder.

"You sure you're not just getting a little on edge?"

"Of course I'm getting edgy. You know me. That's how I roll."

"Well, let's rattle his piñata and see what falls out," Jim said.

E. J. slowed the SUV and pulled over onto the shoulder until the Volvo was forced to go around. Then E. J. pulled out in a chattering spray of gravel and sped up until he was behind the Volvo. "Light them up," he said.

Jim flipped on the flashing red and blue lights.

As soon as he did, the Volvo pulled over abruptly, as though the steering wheel had been jerked.

They both got out, tugging their jackets into place over their shoulder holsters but keeping their hands ready if they needed to go for their guns.

As soon as E. J. looked inside the car, he knew they'd made a mistake. The guy was a mousy fellow with glasses, greying hair, and a receding hairline.

The woman beside him was leaning closer toward them and peering at their faces.

"What's the matter, officers? Was he doing something wrong?" the woman said from the passenger seat.

"No, I guess not," E. J. said. "But maybe if he wouldn't drive like someone's pregnant grandmother, we wouldn't have bothered."

"He does that, officers. He'll glue himself to another car and follow along like we're the caboose in a train. Does it a lot, and I tell him not to, but what are ya gonna do?"

The two headed back toward the SUV, leaving the driver to his personal version of hell.

E. J.'s cell phone rang. He took it out and took a step or two away to answer it.

When he put it away, Jim saw a smile struggling to bust loose on E. J.'s face.

"What?" Jim asked.

"Our guys just got a blip from one of the phones. Someone called one of this Quinn guy's bunch. They'll send the coordinates to us."

"Think we ought to tell Bradley about this?"

"Not just yet." E. J. grinned. "We say too much, and we'll have way too much pain-in-the-butt supervision going on."

They broke into a run and got back into the SUV. E. J. put the vehicle into gear and peeled out around the Volvo, which was still sitting there. The two inside, with arms waving, were hashing out something between them.

"It's showtime," Jim said, feeling the first burst of enthusiasm he'd experienced in a while.

Chapter Eighteen

Al lifted the thick white ceramic mug of coffee and took a sip. *Incredible.* The coffee tasted good.

Last night's reasonable-rate motel could have been anywhere in America—sand-colored heating/air-conditioning unit under the curtained windows, television, king-sized bed, and a bathroom with the usual shampoos, shower caps, and soap the size of a book of matches.

But this diner was a find.

The outside had shown off the rounded chrome of a railroad dining car, with bright red, green, and yellow neon signs. The inside had broad black and white tiles across the floor, red stools in a line along the counter, and red Naugahyde booths. An always-on jukebox played softer oldies tunes. The wall behind the grill and coffee urns sparkled with silvery metal panels, and the pleasant smells had just about knocked them down when they'd entered.

Fergie was looking around at the people who nearly filled every table as well as the row of stools along the counter.

The waitress, a lanky blond, "Call me Phyllis," slid plates in front of them—western omelets, hash browns, OJ, and four rashers of bacon each.

"I love little places like this," Fergie said. "Someday when we're not out fighting crime as a dynamic duo, why don't we drive across America seeking out places just like this? Some could be along some saltwater shore, others within sight of mountains."

"Sounds like an excellent plan. I'm on board."

"Really? You'd leave behind your bass boat and house by the lake for a spell?"

"And crying baby. By that, I mean Maury."

"You don't really mind all that."

"No, I don't, which surprises me."

She looked like she was about to say something but took a bite of omelet instead.

He picked up a slice of bacon. "You're looking quite rosy cheeked and happy today."

"I think you know why."

"Oh my God. You're pregnant?"

She laughed. "You know better than that. But I am enjoying some of our bouncing around through the nooks and crannies of Texas."

"You want to talk about nooks and crannies..."

"Oh, cut it out." But she was chuckling and blushing a little.

He tasted his omelet. *Oh my gosh, this is good.* "We may have to move closer to here," he said.

"Stay with our rolling exploration idea." She looked out the diner's windows at traffic going by. "I'm not even sure I know where 'here' is. We've been so many places."

Al put his fork down and leaned closer. "I have to admit that much of this feels like we're thrashing around guessing and not getting anywhere for all our effort."

"Oh, Al..."

He held up a hand. "What if my assumption that Cynthia probably stayed in Texas is wrong? Hell, we may have a better chance of spotting a chupacabra than we do of tracking down Cynthia and the cancer fund's money."

She reached out to put a hand over his. "I know you think sharing self-doubt makes you more vulnerable and hence attractive. But I would be okay with the exuberant, overconfident Al right now."

He laughed. "Okay. I'll turn off the sad violins. Now tuck into what may be the best food we'll have for a spell."

"I will say it hands down beats breakfast bars and beef jerky."

THEY HAD BARELY STOWED their few things and climbed into the car when Al's cell phone rang.

"Who can that be? Almost no one has your number."

"*Almost* being the operative word. Clayton does now."

He lifted the phone and answered the call. "What can I do you for?"

"How are you coming along with that chupacabra favor I asked of you?"

"This is turning out to be one elusive damn critter." Al caught an eye roll from Fergie.

"Something's elusive all right. I had a couple of FBI agents drop by, asking about you. Seems you gave them the slip."

"I've still got it, haven't I?"

"On the mythical-creature front, I did hear from that goat lady out near the county line."

"Flora-Ida?"

"That's the one. Marvin, one of our newer animal-control people, has been getting some first-rate footage of coyotes, armadillos, skunks, porcupines, possums, and every other creature known to man, but no chupacabra."

"I could have predicted that."

"But even Marvin's tour of the local fauna slowed down when that gal did as you said and got her a jenny, a sassy older one. Not a coyote has come near her goat spread since. And she's sure quit complaining about any damned chupacabra."

"Glad to hear the simple things still work," Al said. "Did you get her name?"

"Whose name?"

"The mule's."

"No. Why?"

"I'd just like to know her name."

"Call her anything you like," Clayton said.

"How's Clarabelle?"

Clayton ignored that. "You know I hear from quite a few other folks in law enforcement out there, at all levels. I have lunch every other month or so with the Austin captain of the attorney general's office here. We have some quite engaging chats. A lot is going on, and it sounds chaotic. In the past, where there has been chaos, I usually find you at the center of it."

"You can always count on me."

"I was afraid of that. Just keep things sensible and me informed. Got that?"

"Okeydokey." Al hung up.

"How's the sheriff?"

"Tetchy, as usual."

"You have a strange relationship with your ex-boss," Fergie said.

"That's me." He glanced at her. "I specialize in strange relationships."

"You'll get no argument from me on that."

Chapter Nineteen

Al's cell phone rang again. He hadn't gotten a call for ages, then suddenly the thing was ringing off the hook, if it had a hook. He glanced toward Fergie and reached for the phone. The caller ID simply said "B" for Bonnie, so it was an in-group call.

"Go ahead. It's your dime," he said.

"It's Maury," Bonnie said, with a little gasp in her voice, as if she'd just run to the phone. "He was supposed to call every day."

"And?"

"He didn't."

"Maybe he remembered that he wasn't supposed to be calling you unless you were using your burner phone, and he can't know that I got it to you."

She didn't say anything.

"You tried to call *him*, didn't you?"

A more demure, "Yeah."

"Maybe he had to turn it off because people were around."

"I don't like it," Bonnie said. "I'm twitchy as all get-out, and I just plain don't like it."

"Okay. I'll try to do something about it."

While he put his phone away, Fergie said, "What if Maury stumbled across Cynthia?"

"Doubtful."

"Maybe we got lucky."

"Yeah. Right. Luck," Al said. "What seems more likely and worries me is if he did something clumsy that gave himself away. Bonnie said he mentioned two big goons there on the ranch."

Nobody was coming in either direction. He turned the car around in a big sweeping U-turn.

"So we're not going to follow that lead about a child-abuse defense charity getting ripped off?"

"It sure sounded like a possibility for someone like Cynthia, but it'll have to wait for now." He pressed on the accelerator and got the Civic up to a near roar.

"Where are we going?"

"My once-troublesome brother may be in trouble."

"So it's his younger brother to the rescue again?"

"Hell, I may have put him in the spot he's in. Might as well get him out, unless it's just a false alarm on Bonnie's part."

At the first chance he got, when a wide gravel patch opened to the right side of the road, he pulled over into it. He got out, went around to the trunk, and came back carrying the small brown canvas duffel bag Sweeting had donated to their cause when he'd loaned them the guns and other stuff inside the bag.

"Just a false alarm, eh?" Fergie said.

"Well, you never know about these things, and it's best not to take chances. If something happens to Maury, I'm going to have a helluva bother getting another brother like him."

"I'm pretty sure the mold got broken when he was made," Fergie agreed.

Al pressed hard on the gas and kept an eye out for cops, which always felt peculiar to him since he'd once been one.

MAURY HEARD NO KNOCK, just a key turning in the thick door.

The door swung open. Luther led the way with Cynthia right behind him. Sean squeezed in next. Maury could see Junior standing just outside the door as it closed.

Maury's insides started running around like rabid mice wanting to get out. He wished he could say something clever that showed he was calm. But his mouth didn't seem to want to work at all for the moment.

In the small room, Sean looked even bigger than he did outside, a black man of solid muscle who glowered in an almost eager way.

Luther and Cynthia sat down on the bare mattress across from Maury, who had stayed seated on his bed.

"Perhaps you already know Candice Styvenghaust here."

"Is that... is that really your name?"

"We all get in the mood for a little name change now and then, Toby," she said. "Or should I say Maury."

Maury's feet felt frozen to the floor and his mouth just as iced shut.

Luther nodded, seeming to understand. "You know, I'm not a violent man by nature. People would call me more clever than physical. But I can have things done to people, have them done quickly and painfully. And here's the thing. It doesn't seem to bother me at all. Do you suppose I might be some sort of psychopath?"

"I don't know," Maury managed. "It kind of hints at that."

That got a chuckle out of both Luther and Cynthia. The expression on Sean's face didn't change in the least.

Luther said, "I'm going to tell you something important that I doubt you could find out on your own."

"Why?" Maury asked.

"Why is it important?"

"No. Why tell me?"

"Call it a whimsy. Also because it isn't likely to matter in your case."

Maury couldn't recall when he'd heard words that chilled him that much.

Cynthia nodded but let Luther do the talking.

"Probably the single thing I stress most here is how not to get caught," Luther said. "The first rule of that is not to do anything that is *per se* illegal."

"But I'll bet you tiptoe pretty close to the line. How about those you teach? Do they ever cross that line?" Maury glanced toward Cynthia.

"The people who leave here are their own responsibility once they walk out the door."

He gave Maury a chance to talk, but Maury didn't feel up to taking it.

"If you've been following the news"—Luther glanced around at the bare room—"though I doubt you've had a chance to do so, you'd know that a couple near Houston just got hauled in. This is a couple who were doing fine and could have stayed legal, but their greed got the best of them, and they got tempted to run a Ponzi-scheme swindle that hardly ever flies these days after all the recent exposure of other failed such efforts."

"Life is about learning," Cynthia said, speaking for the first time.

Luther gave half a shrug. "So, sure, sometimes students like Ollie and Sylvia cross lines. My first lesson to them is not to do so. But there are those who misconstrue my level of involvement or responsibility. It's the reason I've brought in a couple of temporary hires like Sean and Junior."

"Somebody who claims to have cartel connections might have taken umbrage," Cynthia said.

"Now, now. No need to share too much." Luther ran a finger inside the neck of his mock turtleneck shirt. "But I do teach from experience. While I am being careful not to scam cartels, I did pick the wrong person. I thought the woman was old and helpless. She was a tough cow lady from around Fort Worth. You should have seen her. She was as stocky as the cattle on her big spread in the Seguin area. She wore jeans, cowboy boots, pearl-button shirts, and rode horses. I took her for almost a million. She had lots more. Yet she vowed to string me up or get someone to do it who knew how."

"It's hard to tell if her cartel threat had anything to it," Cynthia said. "But someone with her kind of money might almost certainly have the ear of law enforcement at the state level."

"Tut tut," Luther said. "I think we're beginning to worry Maury."

Maury could have said he was plenty worried already if he'd been able to speak.

Luther leaned closer. "Are we? Enough for you to tell who's in this with you?"

"Besides your wife, who probably is, he means," Cynthia said.

"One minute you say you seek to stay legal, the next you threaten me and my wife," Maury managed to say. "How about your holding me against my will? Isn't that a form of kidnapping? That seems a nudge or two over that delicate line."

"Our original thinking was to keep you otherwise occupied until Candice here could go far, far away."

"But now?" Maury had to ask.

"Well, you see, as of this moment, I don't think anyone can prove you're here or that you haven't already left on your own. I have deniability... if it comes to that."

"What are you going to do with me?"

"I'm still deciding."

"Wouldn't killing me cross some line?"

"Well, there are lines and there are lines. Most of what I do is in the lineless grey areas of life. But if I need to cross one, I'll do it like taking a speedway over the Rubicon."

Chapter Twenty

Al drove by the front of the place at a little after two in the morning.

"Doesn't look like much of an active cattle ranch." Fergie looked up at the arched wooden sign that said Charles P Ranch as they went past.

"The good news there is that maybe we won't end up stepping into cow pies, although we might be stepping into something far worse. I'd rather do this on my own."

"You're taking me with you," she said. "We agreed on that."

"Only after an argument that lasted a hundred miles, and one I was doomed to lose anyway."

He drove around for twenty minutes before he found a spot where he could back into a thick clutter of sage and stands of prickly-pear cactus high enough to hide the car. He got out and used a fallen limb to brush away the tire tracks leading from the road to where he'd hidden the Civic.

When he got back to the car, Fergie was digging around in the canvas bag. She held up half a dozen plastic zip-strip handcuffs, what they used to call wrist ties or riot cuffs back when they were active. An officer could slip them in his or her cap, and they were disposable though harder than hell to cut.

"Sure," Al said. "Take whatever you think you'll need and are willing to carry."

He took out the shotgun then slipped it back inside the bag. It would make far too much noise and was a close-up weapon at best. He had his Sig Sauer, and Fergie took the Ruger.

"In a perfect world, we wouldn't need to use either," Al said. "We'll be in and out of there, hopefully with Maury in tow. I just hope we don't find him sleeping soundly and safely while he's just forgotten to call."

"I don't know. You said Bonnie seemed pretty worried."

Fergie looked around. Though it was dark, she could make out a cattle fence ahead. All they needed to do was climb that and head for the house and watch for rattlesnakes, which might be actively hunting, as warm as the nights had been. They were apt to see other critters as well, from porcupines to skunks to armadillos. Hell, they might even run into a damn chupacabra. She would have chuckled if she wasn't already tensing up inside.

Al led the way to the fence. He climbed over first and waited to make sure Fergie got across as easily, a gesture she appreciated. The stars looked bright and closer to the ground. The moon seemed to have grown some, enough to cast shadows but not to light up the ground all the way clearly. They wove their way through clumps of prickly pear, sage, and an occasional mesquite tree. The land had been cleared long ago, but vegetation was growing back in where it hadn't kicked up its toes and turned brown in the drought.

The ranch house was quite a bit farther back than Fergie had counted on. When first she spotted it and its few outbuildings, she could see few lights and no activity. That was good.

Al moved closer and whispered in her ear, "Maury is likely to be in the bunkhouse. Let's start there."

Al led her around through the parking lot so that they would have the cover of the various vehicles as they crept forward. They passed a toolshed and picnic table, moving closer into the shadows of the buildings to slink toward the front door.

Someone was sitting on a tilted-back chair by the bunkhouse's front door, a big someone, a big black someone. It figured the place would be guarded if something was up. Fergie glanced to Al, who pointed toward the back of the building.

They went around that way but found no rear door. That was odd. Still moving, they eased back up to the front again. Fergie peeked around. The chair was empty. Maybe the guard had heard the call of nature or even gone off to bed. She signaled for Al to hurry. She took off toward the door.

As soon as she got there, she tried the knob. The door was unlocked. That saved them a lot of bother. She shot inside. Al came in right behind her and closed the door quietly.

This foyer hallway led to a T. She peeked around the corner. Rooms with closed doors ran along either side. It didn't look like any bunkhouse she'd ever seen before.

Al pointed down to the right, where an empty chair sat outside one door.

He got to it and tested it, and it opened. She'd been hoping to see him get out his lockpick kit and have a go at it. Then she remembered the kit was back in the gun safe at Al's lakeside house.

She rushed inside the room as soon as Al was inside. She reached and flipped on the light switch. A single bulb hanging from its cord at the center of the ceiling lit the room.

"Al! Fergie!" Maury yelled. "Watch out!"

A huge muscled white guy with a buzz cut sat up from where he'd been lying stretched out on the striped bare mattress of the room's other bed. He scrambled to his feet and charged toward Al.

Al ducked low under the rush. As the man went past, Al put a hard elbow into the man's kidney, but the big guy didn't stagger. He merely spun and rushed toward Al again.

Al was quicker on his feet than the bigger man expected. He also knew the secret of pressure points and spots where even a man as big as this was vulnerable.

The man swung a fist at Al but caught air while Al rushed in, pummeling blows to a solar plexus that sounded as weak as the thick metal side of a battleship.

Al switched to a pressure grip to the man's hand that lifted him up onto his toes while Al hit him three times with the other hand, each time hitting a spot that made the man buckle like an accordion.

Fergie eased around to the side wall, to be out of the way.

MAURY HAD BEEN AS SURPRISED as the big lumpy Junior when Al and Fergie came into the room. He watched Al take on a man who looked three times bigger, doing so with confidence. Maury had seen Al fight before and knew he would use his feet, special holds, even anything unfair, all faster than his opponents expected from a guy Al's age.

Junior had started the scuffle with a smirk, but that soon changed into wonder, and perhaps the tiniest bit of fear. Every move he made seemed bulky and at a slower speed, while Al moved around and scored again and again with blows to the right places, finally catching him in a field-goal-worthy punt to the crotch that dropped Junior to his knees. Al rushed in and chop, chop, chopped to the neck. Junior's movements slowed, but he didn't go down. So Al moved around to close in from behind. He locked his arms around Junior's oversized neck in a choke submission hold. Junior reached up as if in slow motion to slap at Al's arms. The third time his hands went up, they didn't make it all the way to Al's arms, instead stopping and slowly dropping. Junior's eyes lost their focus, and he wobbled then fell forward.

Maury's eyes bulged, and he bent closer to feel for a pulse on Junior's neck. He let out a sigh when he felt one. "I cannot believe you were ever able to do that."

"Later, Maury. We need to get a move on."

Maury would have cheered, but the door opened, and a blur came up behind Al. One big black hand curled around Al's neck, then another. They lifted him off the ground until his feet kicked uselessly in the air. His face started to turn purple. He beat his fists at the hands holding him by the throat, but they didn't let go.

In a second or two, it would be over. Then Sean gave a lurch, twitched again, then let go of Al's neck.

Al dropped to the floor, gasping and gulping for air. Sean stood with a bewildered look that turned blank. Twitching, he fell forward onto the floor across Junior's body.

Still gasping for air, Al stepped in to tap Sean all the way out with the butt of his gun.

Maury could see something black in Fergie's hand, recognizing a Taser now that he looked closer.

"I didn't know you brought that thing along," Al said with a raspy voice while rubbing his throat.

"I like to think I bring the electricity to this relationship."

"I'll go along with that," Al said. "Now let me have a few of those ties."

They used up all the dozen plastic zip-strip handcuffs they had binding the wrists and ankles of the big guys. Then they stepped around them and headed for the door. Fergie held up a key she'd taken from Sean.

"You know, that Cynthia woman is here somewhere on the grounds," Maury said.

"That'll have to wait until another day," Al said. "Right now, we have one priority, and that's to get you the hell out of here."

"I'm okay with that." Maury swung the room's door open, then he took a slow step back.

"What the hell...?" Al started to say.

Maury saw Luther standing in the doorway, holding a pistol leveled at them in his right hand. Behind him, Cynthia and Charlie were peering into the room, looking down at the two giants trussed on the floor.

Chapter Twenty-One

Al could see enough of the gun in Luther's hand to know it was a Walther PPK. It looked like the 7.65mm model, not the easiest pistol to get ammo for these days but lethal enough to poke holes in anyone. Luther held it without any shake to his hand, and if he thought it made him seem like James Bond, he wasn't allowing himself to be swept away by the fantasy. His eyes were all business, and he kept the barrel pointed at Al's belly button.

"Carefully put your weapons on the floor," he said.

He stepped into the room, closer. He couldn't miss. Cynthia and Charlie crowded in to either side of him, Cynthia to his right, Charlie to his left. This was Al's first time seeing Cynthia. With the white hair and nursing-home uniform, she looked almost kind until she smiled, which was with the bared teeth of a wolf. Like any good con artist, she could be an actress full time around others, those whom she sought to bamboozle. But not now.

Al took his Sig Sauer out from behind his back where he'd returned it and lowered it to the floor. He was thinking as hard and fast as he could but couldn't see any good or happy way out of this.

Fergie glanced toward Al as she bent to place the Ruger on the floor.

"I was hoping to resolve your presence with no violence," Luther said to Maury. "But just look at the mess your friends have made of things."

"Yep. Too late now," Charlie said. His face lit up in unabashed glee.

"You can't do this. I've got to get back to—"

Whatever Maury was going to say got punctuated by a full swing of a backhand across his face from Cynthia. "Oh, how I've been wanting to do that," she said. Her face twisted into a snarl. "Ever since you showed up here, where I thought I was safe."

Fergie started to rush to Maury's side.

"Stay right where you are, all of you." Luther spoke from between clenched teeth. It wouldn't take much for him to pull the trigger.

They froze.

"This is a soundproofed room, as you've probably already figured out."

Maury struggled to get to his feet again.

Cynthia swung her right hand high over her left shoulder and brought it down in another smashing backhand that sent Maury flying backward onto his fanny, sliding across the floor a foot or two.

"That one just *felt* good," she said.

Al expected Maury to stay down for the count after that blow. He was wrong.

Maury surged up from the floor like some wild animal, smashing head-on into Cynthia's midriff. Caught off guard, she tumbled back into Luther, who was trying to reach around her to get a shot at Maury.

Bam. The gun went off.

Al whooshed in, kicking upward. The gun flew out of Luther's hand. Luther tried to grab for it.

Al grabbed Luther's wrist with both hands and whirled, pushing hard on the back of the hand with his thumbs.

As Luther's body twisted around, trying to keep up with his arm, the bones of his fingers and hands crackled as several of them broke all at once.

The gun clattered to the floor. Charlie bent and scrambled for it, but Fergie kicked, catching him just under the chin. His beard might have cushioned some of the blow, but the kick lifted him off his feet to crash into the far wall. She stepped in close and hit him twice in the stomach as hard as she could. He bent double and threw up on the floor.

Al had Luther's hand twisted up behind his back while Luther was up on his tiptoes and screaming. Al glanced toward Cynthia, who had dropped to the floor with both hands on her side. Blood was seeping from between her fingers. She looked up at Al then Maury, her eyes puzzled then slowly fading to blank. She toppled onto her side.

"Ah, ah, ah! Take anything you want." Luther's screaming made Al wonder just how soundproofed the room was.

Fergie picked up her Ruger. She stepped close and tapped its long barrel hard against Luther's temple. The first time didn't work, so she did it again, harder. That ended the screaming.

Al stepped back, letting Luther fall to the floor beside Cynthia.

Maury bent over Cynthia and put two fingers on her neck. He looked up at Al and shook his head then changed his mind and nodded. "Just fainted, I think. I hope."

The only other sound in the room was Charlie's retching and gasping. The room was beginning to take on an unpleasant smell.

Fergie went to the bed where Maury had slept. She yanked the sheet off and tore it into long strips. She wadded one piece up and tied the others together. Maury helped her by holding Cynthia up enough so Fergie could press the clump of cloth against the entrance and exit wounds of the through-and-through shot, which looked to have grazed her hip bone.

"She was lucky, damned lucky," Fergie said. "Luther had no idea what he was doing, waving that damned gun around."

"Yeah. Lucky. That's her all right." Maury looked at Cynthia's closed eyes and calm face.

Al thought that passed out like this was the first time she looked like she wasn't ready to bite someone. She'd probably looked sweet and nice enough when she was working her con, especially the senior-care-center nurse one. But he'd not had the opportunity to witness her when she was playing nice.

Fergie finished wrapping the torn sheet strips around Cynthia's torso so that they could apply pressure on the wounds. She tied off the knots, then she and Maury maneuvered Cynthia into an upright sitting position against the wall.

Al bent to pick up his pistol and Luther's PPK. He tucked his Sig Sauer at the small of his back again. He handed the PPK to Maury. "Hang on to this but be reluctant to use it."

Maury nodded. His face was flushed red on the side where Cynthia had belted him a couple of times, but other than feeling around with his tongue to see if his teeth were loose, he seemed more cheerful than Al expected.

Fergie and Maury stood over Cynthia. "Do you want to kick her or anything?" Fergie asked Maury.

"Naw. But I'm sure hoping to ask her about the money, though. Not getting it back may cost Bonnie and me our jobs at the hospital."

As if to punctuate his sentence, an alarm started to sound in a strident blare, like a car alarm, only much louder.

"Oh, my auntie's fanny," Maury said. "What now?"

"How many others are there here who could be headed this way just now?" Al asked.

"I don't know. I don't know." Maury's eyes were open as wide as possible.

"Then we have to get out of here. Pronto," Al said.

"But the money?"

"We can't risk it. We have a slightly higher priority at the moment, like getting you the hell out of here. We don't have time to wait around for you to question her," Al said, "as much as it *is* kind of the thrust of our mission since we've found her."

"I... I know," Maury said.

"We don't know what triggered the alarm," Fergie said. "Probably not anybody in this room. We can't stay and take a chance, Maury."

"Then let's scoot." Al looked down at Cynthia, Candice, Cat, or whatever the hell her name really was. "At least we were successful in our hunt, kind of."

"Well, we sure enough found her all right," Fergie said. "She's right there, Maury. Sure you don't want to give her some of your toe?"

"No. I just want to go home," Maury said.

"Check them all for keys," Al said.

After she'd poked through their pockets, Fergie said, "Luther had one. Now we have the only two."

"That's the way we want it," Al said.

Maury opened the door, and Al and Fergie backed out, keeping an eye on those inside. No one inside the room made a move.

"Whew," Maury said as Fergie used the key to lock the door from the outside. She put it in her pocket instead of leaving it in the door. "That should buy us enough time for a getaway."

Only a few of the doors along the hallway had opened. Some of the male scam-school students were in their pajamas or other nightwear and looked around, reluctant to leap into anything like a fire drill. But others had tugged on clothes. They came bursting out of their rooms at a run. The others slipped back inside to change.

Al took off at a near run, mingling with those heading for the front door, and Fergie was right behind him.

Maury stayed close as they headed down the hallway and started out the front door. All the people stirred inside the bunkhouse, and more lights flipped on in the ranch house. One or two of its doors opened just as Al scooted out of the building.

As they stepped clear of the building, the alarm grew far louder than a car alarm, approaching a hysterical level. Al still didn't know if other security people would come charging their way at any moment.

But it would be a while at least before anyone could locate and free those locked back in that room.

Al ran across the open area, lit up now as more lights came on. He, Maury, and Fergie ducked in close to the side of the toolshed, where heavy shadows masked them.

More people poured from the front of the bunkhouse, probably the ones who had taken time to dress. A few females were emerging from the back of the ranch house. They all looked far from organized and didn't seem to have any idea what was going on. It could have been a fire drill for all they knew. Some of those standing outside were in bathrobes or held blankets around their shoulders. Soon, they were all gathering in clumps and talking.

Since none of them seemed too diligent or capable of looking about, and no one who looked like more security had charged out of the ranch house, Al signaled the others, and they bent low and started out through the parking lot.

Chapter Twenty-Two

The usual night lights around the ranch were on, but the grounds were quieter the farther they got from that persistent alarm. Fergie looked back. Some people were scurrying around but with no clear purpose. They looked like ants from a disturbed anthill. No one seemed to be following them. Still, she stayed crouched low like the other two. The sky seemed unusually black to Fergie. Only splinters of light showed here and there near the buildings.

The three of them were weaving through the parking lot when Fergie said, "I'm glad we got Maury out of there, but it's sure a shame we couldn't do anything about getting the money back."

"Hey, wait a minute, you guys," Maury said.

"What?" Al stopped and looked all around.

"This cab driver from Iraq was telling me how in a war-torn country like that, they use banks less and keep their cash in vehicles that move about," Maury said.

"Gripping story, but what's your point?" Al asked. "We need to move."

"The point is that Cynthia has the same vehicle she had when working the hospital scam, only it's been repainted. Why not just get a different vehicle? Maybe she's learned something from her Rom friends and wants to keep her nest egg close."

"Point us there," Al said.

He led them to the June bug–green Town & Country minivan. "I figure someone like Cynthia who changes identity a lot has no need for Social Security, especially if she has a big pile of cash set aside. It probably has to be mobile too if she moves around a lot. Where else to keep it but in her car? She has different tags, but that's all."

Al tried the doors. They were all locked. "Any ideas, guys?"

"The toolshed," Maury said. "Maybe there's something there. It's our best shot."

Fergie felt every sense she had intensified. Her ears screamed, trying to hear running footsteps responding to that blasted alarm. Her legs wanted her to run. But she followed along as Al and Maury slipped into the tool room.

"A coat hanger, anything." Al moved a shovel and rake to look behind them. He looked behind the weight bench and the weights.

The room looked neat and orderly, but Fergie couldn't see anything they could use to open a vehicle.

"Ah, wait," Maury said.

He went to the doorway and reached up above the inside doorjamb. His hand came out holding up a slim jim, the kind used to slide inside car doors to pop the lock.

"Brilliant," Fergie said. "How did you know to find it there?"

"I figured they'd have one, being the kind of people they are, and then I just had to think about where I'd keep it."

They hurried back to the Town & Country. Al slid the slim jim down inside the glass and rubber on the driver's side door. He fiddled about for a while. At last, something clicked, and the lock inside popped up.

"The thing about a vehicle like this," he said as he swung the door open and released the side door and slid it back, "is that they have a number of regular hiding spots in addition to some you can make."

He popped the nearest seat back and opened what looked like a trap door. Fergie leaned closer, heard Maury gasp, and saw green bundles of bills stacked neatly, hundreds.

"How much do you think is in this vehicle?" Maury said.

"No idea," Al said, "but we're not going to take the time to check now. At least we don't have to walk out of here."

"But we have no key," Maury said.

"Hop in and give me a moment," Al said.

While they got inside, opening and closing the doors as quietly as they could, Al's hands were under the steering column. He pulled out some wires, stripped a couple of them, and rubbed them together. The engine caught and started. He twisted the wires together and let them hang.

"Let's get out of here," he said.

He drove slowly and carefully.

Fergie's nerves were screaming now, expecting to hear a yell and to see people come rushing out.

But Al took them calmly up the drive. Once on the road, he drove to where they had left the Civic.

While Maury and Fergie were getting out of the Town & Country, Al hurried to the Civic and popped the trunk. He came running back to them, carrying the canvas bag. "Give me all the guns and the Taser, and I'll put them in here. Give me the Walther you have too, Maury."

"But why? We may need them," Fergie said.

"Just do it, for now, and hurry. I'll drive the minivan."

She'd known him long enough not to argue. She went to the Civic and got behind the wheel. Maury climbed into the passenger seat.

Al fussed around inside the minivan for a couple moments then came running over to them, put the canvas bag in their trunk, and gave them a short wave. He ran all the way back to the minivan.

As soon as he was inside, Fergie pulled out onto the road. Al followed along behind.

For the very first time in a long time, Fergie took in a full breath. The oxygen felt rich and calming as it coursed through her. A tiny dome of light shone in the black sky over what must have been the ranch behind them, and it faded as they rolled down the road. They'd done it. They'd gotten away.

"ARE WE STILL HEADED the right direction?" E. J. asked.

Jim was looking down at the laptop he held. "I'm getting a pretty clear bead here. Shouldn't be too much farther ahead," he said. "This was the only phone-call ping we had from that Quinn guy's bunch."

"We'll have something for Bradley soon enough if I have anything to say about it." E. J.'s hands clenched the steering wheel more tightly.

The two of them had met during their Quantico training. E. J. was short for Enoch James Scholling, while Perkins's whole name was James Robert Perkins. When their boss, Benjamin Omar Bradley, first saw that, he started calling them Jim One and Jim Two, which secretly infuriated both of them. Then he came up with something worse. With their builds and matching haircuts, they'd looked enough alike to be called twins. Bradley had picked up on that and called them "my boys," as if they were his own damned twin children.

He took almost as much pride in their track record as they did, took credit for it himself when he could, and let them carry any blame when things didn't go just right. He had several two-person teams like theirs out pursuing every lead in such a high-profile case. When they said they wanted to stake out the witnesses, Bradley had said, "Go for it, but..."

"We know."

"Say it," Collins encouraged.

They had looked to each other. Jim finally said, "Don't call for back-up until we have an actual sighting this time."

Their record was good but not perfect.

"Make one mistake, and then it's this sort of thing from the boss," E. J. had said once they'd left Bradley's office.

"It's always about budget," Jim said. "Wasn't our fault our targets slipped away before the tactical squad arrived."

"If our targets had ever been there."

"Oh, they were there, just gone when it mattered. A lot of wasted money, according to Bradley."

"This time, we'll make damn sure we have an ironclad ID, even if each has to be made from a corpse," Jim said.

"Are you positive that our two shooters will go after the witnesses?" E. J. asked.

"No. But I'm pretty sure. It makes sense and fits with their past. They finish things. Lee Fenston made his way back to his unit, carrying his dead best friend. He's no quitter." Jim looked up from his laptop. "And Garson McBallister has more decorations than Fenston."

"Why don't they just take off, stay in the wind?"

"I'm banking that they think they have unfinished business," Jim said. "And, like I said..."

E. J. pressed on the gas, taking them twenty miles per hour over the speed limit.

Jim couldn't see any vehicles around them in any direction. *Good.* He thought of himself as the more dependable and clear thinking of them. But when it came to muscle and plain stupid daring, he had to tip his hat to E. J.

"But that Quinn fellow and his string-bean red-headed friend didn't get a clear make on them. Their testimony would be worthless in court."

"These guys don't know that. Besides, this nurse friend of theirs, Bonnie, took out their pal Brandon Highwater. They might want to do her just for that." Jim closed his laptop and put it back in its case.

"Yeah. These are sure two twitchy guys." The thought made E. J. grin.

"And with damn all in the way of training."

"Okay. Where is it?" E. J. asked.

"Way the hell on the other side of the county, of course. But at least it's close to a lake."

"That'll just mean mosquitoes," Jim said.

"They'll be the least of our worries if those two we're looking for show up armed the way they are."

"We'll have a little something waiting on them."

Jim was referring to the two MP5/40s in their cases in the back of the SUV. These Heckler & Koch submachine models were chambered for .40-caliber Smith & Wesson cartridges—not the standard FBI weapon, but an old favorite of theirs, with thirty-round polymer box magazines.

"They pack plenty of punch and should stand up well if those guys are still carrying AR-15s."

"You know we're not to engage them unless we have to."

"Yeah." E. J. chuckled. "When Bradley himself is out here taking heavy fire, we'll give him a chance to rethink that. In the meantime, I'm going to be carrying all the extra clips I can."

Chapter Twenty-Three

Fergie was breathing easily and regularly again, glad to get away from there clear, when she went around a slow bend in the otherwise deserted road. Swirling blue and red lights suddenly lit up around them.

"Oh, what fresh hell is this?" Maury said.

Troopers in uniform waved them off the road. Fergie looked all around and saw several state-trooper vehicles and thus had no alternative. She'd been on the other side of the lights many times, but not this time, and it didn't feel good—not good at all. A lump rose into her chest and stayed there. When she turned off the engine and lifted her hands from the steering wheel, they were shaking.

She opened the door.

"Step out of the vehicle," the trooper nearest her said.

Maury was already out the other side and looked ready to do whatever they said, put his hands on the vehicle and get patted down, whatever.

Al sauntered up to the Civic, with a trooper on either side of him.

Once she was standing outside the car, Fergie could make out one darker car among the three state vehicles.

"Oh, my stars," she said, thinking that this was a lot of cars for a traffic stop.

From out of the dark, still in a suit, strolled Sidney Draper of the attorney general's office.

He smiled at Al. "We meet again."

"So we do," Al said.

Draper held out the flat of his hand, palm up.

"I'd give you the keys, but you know..." Al glanced toward Fergie.

The red and blue lights swept across Al's face like some psychedelic splashes of color at a disco club. She didn't know what to make of the expression on his face, though she might not have been seeing it as clearly as she thought. Fergie could swear he was suppressing a smile.

"Right. You had to hotwire it." Sidney waved to one of the troopers, who went over to the minivan, hopped inside, and took off down the highway.

"Is there anything inside that will please me?" Sidney asked.

"Lots."

"I'll say this," Sidney said. "That Cat is one heck of a rainmaker. But this time, she's heading for a stormy patch."

"That she was," Al agreed. "She already got a bit of that. You might want to call for an EMS too. She took a bullet."

"You did that?"

"No. Luther did." Fergie remembered hearing Luther's fingers crackle like peanut brittle as they broke. And the two big thugs were probably the worse for wear as well.

"Come to think of it," Al said, "there may be more than one who needs a little EMS attention."

Al held out his key to Room 17, with its number on it. "You may need this. It'll save you having to break down the door."

Sidney took the key. "Do you want to make something of the kidnapping thing?"

"Not unless you need it," Al said.

"I doubt it. We expect to get plenty enough on our own. But I'll let you know."

"Okay."

"We have some other business now," Sidney said. "I trust you'll understand."

"Fine with me," Al said. "Power to you."

"You'd best be scooting. Things are about to get lively around here."

Then Sidney did something that surprised Fergie more than anything he'd done before. He held out a hand. Al reached out and shook it.

"You're free to go," Sidney said.

While the troopers all got back into their cruisers and turned off their flashing lights, which had been quite a show, Al got into the driver's seat of the Civic as the troopers all pulled away and headed back toward the ranch.

"Hop in, guys," Al said.

While Maury scrambled into the back seat, Fergie slid more slowly into the passenger seat. "What the hell was that, Al?"

"That was us getting away with rescuing Maury," he said.

"But the money?" Maury said.

Al shrugged. "What we have to do is think about Bonnie now and the baby and Tanner. Those two men who want to kill Fergie and me are still on the loose. The only link they may have to us is Bonnie if they were able to trace the call that went to her old cell phone from Maury."

"Do they have the technology to do that?" Maury asked.

"Maybe not. But those FBI guys do."

"You think...?"

"Yes. I think our trigger-happy pals have the skills to follow a couple of Bureau agents around and the sense to do so. I'm almost sure of it."

"Then we'd better get a wiggle on," Fergie said.

LEE FOUND HIMSELF GRIPPING the steering wheel more tightly as they got closer. He made himself relax. "I start asking myself if we don't keep making ourselves challenges because we don't know how to or don't want to quit. Has fighting for our country made us into that?"

Garson reached to rub his forehead and temple like he was getting a migraine. He looked up with that pained expression Lee knew so well. "No." He shook his head. "We just have a taste for it, the killing. It's what we do when we don't know what else to do."

Lee stayed quiet for a long stretch. He was thinking about Brenda and Garson's wife, Ginger, though he'd been told by Garson not to mention her name.

"Forgive and forget," that therapist counselor had said. Well, no one had said that to them while they were overseas laying their lives on the line. If a buddy got shot or blown into sixty-eight pieces, they didn't forgive a damn thing. They went in there, careful mad, and ripped out some veins and danced in the pools of blood.

Brenda had made it worse, of course, by taking the high ground. The senator was the one who had done all the pressuring. All she'd done was cave in, she said, once or twice. Okay, three or four times. What he'd gathered from Garson before he turned into a clam about the whole thing was that his story was pretty much the same.

How in the hell Brenda had started to resent him so was what puzzled Lee most. He'd come back from a tour of duty to find his wife in the middle of the media splash of accusing a US senator of sexual harassment. She admitted to bedding down with the guy. Lee got upset by that, and suddenly it was Lee who was the bad guy. *Incredible.* He could almost picture them at their wedding, talking about loving, cherishing, and most of all, honoring each other. *Then all this shit.*

"Hey, our Bureau guys are slowing down, turning in to a place," Garson said. "I think we've finally located where our witnesses are holed up."

Good. Lee had worked himself up into a right state where he needed to direct his anger and do some serious harm to someone or something. He should have done that to Brenda, but oh no, he'd just walked away. They'd taken out that asshole Bentley, sure enough. *But so what?* Nothing felt good anymore. *Well, maybe this will.*

"We'll go up the road a mile or so and then work our way back in. No sense putting any more stress on your leg than we need to."

"My damn leg is just fine," Garson said. "In a week, I'll be running the hundred meters in the Olympics. I can damn well hobble along for a mile or so readily enough if need be, and we want the cushion."

Lee drove right past the place where Garson was getting the blip on his GPS app. *The Bureau agents are in there.* He couldn't see a building or the black SUV, but they were there, and they were there because of the witnesses Lee and Garson needed to take care of. That meant they'd first have to take care of their little FBI buddies who'd led them here. No extra charge. Then do the witnesses.

The damn brush was so puny, browned and leaves falling out all over the place, that it took him a while to find a place to tuck away the silver Subaru they'd found outside a 7-11 with the keys still in it. Hell, a baby seat was in the back. But they'd jumped at the chance to boost a ride and had the good luck not to get spotted by any trooper or county cop. Luck. They were just dripping with luck. He started to chuckle.

"What's so funny?" Garson asked.

"Everything," Lee said. He pulled the vehicle up close behind the thick trunk of what looked like a pecan or live oak. A stand of brush between where he parked and the road masked the Subaru completely. "Everything's funny right now, and the big joke is going to be on a couple of Bureau guys."

"Hell, I wish they weren't in the mix. The witnesses are gonna be cream puffs. But special agents have a burr under their saddles and are probably just looking to mix it up."

"Then I guess we'll mix it up." Lee turned off the dome light, climbed out his door, and went around to get the AR-15s out of the back. He flipped aside the baby blanket they'd used to cover the weapons.

Each of them strapped on a backpack and took up one of the guns, each with a bump stock. Lee wished they had better, but they might fix that soon enough. "Let's go do this thing," he said.

Garson was already headed that way, breaking into a jog, slight limp and all. Lee took off in a run, feeling the urgency ripple through him, soon passing Garson while making as little sound as possible.

He wanted to get in place as soon as they located the agents, have the edge on those two, and then get all this over with. He'd scrambled plenty when he had goals overseas, and winning here was even more pressing. The one thing he'd taken away from all his experiences was that seconds were strategic, and knowing that had allowed him to accomplish missions and had brought him home alive.

Chapter Twenty-Four

"Pull over somewhere when you get the chance," Jim said.

E. J. slowed, looked each direction into the dark all around them, and eased the SUV off the road. The brush and leaf litter was dry and crackled as he kept going until the vehicle was concealed behind thick stands of mountain cedar that had begun to turn a rusty orange.

"Are we close?" he asked.

"Close enough," Jim said. "I didn't see any spot where our shooter guys already went in, so I think we beat them here."

"Maybe we did. Maybe we didn't. I wouldn't expect them to leave any sign." E. J. turned off the dome light then the engine. "But we expected to get here first. If they aren't here yet, we'll wait on them. If they're here already, somehow we'll find them." He got out and went around to the back of the vehicle, opened the doors, and started to put on his tactical assault gear. He set one of the bulletproof vests aside for Jim.

Jim pulled two thick cases closer and flipped them open to expose the H&Ks, getting them ready before starting to suit up as well. "I thought you had a shot at getting back with Angie," he said.

"Yeah well, that fell through."

"Same stuff?"

"Yep. Married to my work. What a crock. But I wouldn't mind her being there when I come home."

"Women. They're a chore, all right." Jim finished dressing and picked up one of the H&Ks. He jacked a shell into the chamber and flipped the safety. *Locked and loaded.*

"Think we'll even have time to call for backup once we see these guys?"

"Don't know, with the training these guys have had," Jim said. "If we do see these guys, I doubt we'll have enough time to howl at the moon."

"We've had training too," E. J. said. "Might even be a fair fight unless we get the drop on them, which is the way I'd sure like to play it."

"You ever think," Jim asked, "that the only thing separating us from those two is our intentions?"

"I don't know. They probably thought they had good intentions in taking out that senator. Lots of women's groups might agree. I might myself if my wife had been one of those he was jumping."

"You don't have a wife... now."

"Well, I might again someday."

"Lest we talk ourselves to death, let's just go set up before these guys get here." Jim looked around. "I don't welcome a face-to-face go-around with these guys. I want the edge."

"Don't worry." E. J. patted the H&K he held. "We have them out-gunned."

He looked up and saw no moon in sight—no stars either, for that matter. The clouds rolling in for the first time in weeks obscured them. *Perfect.* He felt the night was a fine one for an ambush. He intended to be the one springing any ambush that took place.

Both of the MP5/40 H&Ks were fitted with LED WeaponLights. The batteries gave them an hour and a half to two hours of tactical time, which should be plenty.

Without having to say a thing to each other, they spread out until they were just able to make each other out in the dark. Though Jim wore dark clothing as well, E. J. could make out his silhouette enough to know they were as far apart as they dared. They started in, weaving among the shrubs, trees, and stands of cactus. He was peering hard, watching for the merest hint of movement.

Jim might have seemed to lean on him at times, but E. J. knew he could be counted on, and that was what mattered. They'd been in tough situations before, and each had each other's backs all the way in and out, so far.

The two they were after weren't people to take lightly. Hell, they'd already killed a US senator. They were both battle scarred and experienced from their tours of duty as well.

E. J. knew that once a visual sighting had been made, all he would have to do was give a shout out up the chain of command, and a tactical team would be rushed in here, heavily armed and carrying the best in thermal-imaging devices. *But where would the glory be in that?* They would get all the credit, and he and Jim had worked hard enough already to earn and deserve that. If anyone was going to get a pat on the back for taking down these two rogue killers, it was going to be them.

The damned ground beneath his feet was so dry that it was difficult to take a step without making a rattle or crackle. He slowed, moving the leaves to the side before taking each step.

They'd just arrived and not had time to explore the area. But it was small enough. He knew if he was one of these two, he'd seek the high ground. He felt the ground rising higher to his left and eased that direction. Jim stayed the same distance but followed E. J.'s lead.

Abruptly, he stopped. Ahead he could see the glimmer of lights from a trailer. That was probably the target. He slowed even more. A sloth could have raced past him. He wasn't looking toward the trailer anymore but away from it, where a shooter would naturally want to set up for the best coverage of the open area. The main thing he figured he had going for him was that either of the shooters would be fixed on the trailer. He should have the margin of discovery for a shot, even if it was a second or two.

In the distance, lightning flashed in bursts along the horizon. Thunder sounded in a low rumble that grew gradually louder.

Good. E. J. turned off his weapon's light and moved faster through the crispy leaf litter with the sounds of nature covering up what little noise he made.

THE TWO AGENTS WERE barely out of sight when Garson stepped out from the dense shadows around the trunk of a big live oak. He moved forward with only a slight limp, glancing around as if MPs might pop out next. Being AWOL put him on edge, as if the past few days weren't enough to hone him to an even finer paranoia.

Lee rose up from beneath a cover of leaves, shaking them off as he stood and moved toward the SUV. He was still breathing heavily from the scramble to get into place while those two Bureau dudes were pulling in and settling.

"I could have taken them both out, just like that," Garson said. "Probably should have. Bing. Bing."

"We agreed we needed them to lead us to our witnesses first."

Lee pulled on a black ski mask and handed a spare one to Garson to replace the one he'd lost when that truck had rolled. They'd had the devil's own time buying a few of them at this time of year, hot as it had been. Luckily, that military-surplus store Banana Arms had finally had what they wanted. Now their faces were covered. If they had thought of that before being at Bentley's cabin, they wouldn't have needed to be out here now. *But there you have it!*

"Just the two of them," Garson said. "No backup. Humpf. Guess they want to do things for themselves."

"I like that about them." Lee went over to the SUV. "They're like us."

"Except we're better."

"Way better. This should be a bit of fun." He popped the SUV's doors without setting off an alarm. He reached to open the hood.

Garson came around in a moment holding the distributer cap. "What goodies are you finding in the back?"

"Loads and loads of ammo." Lee opened his backpack and loaded in as much as he could. It didn't match the NATO rounds they had in their AR-15s, but he was planning on getting his hands on one of those H&Ks.

"I don't think they meant just to capture us."

"That's naughty of them."

"Yep. They should be taught a lesson."

"With extreme prejudice?"

"That's what I had in mind."

"The colonel used to say that a lot. He said it once while he was blowing a guy's brain all over a stucco wall."

"Yeah. Yeah. Now remember," Garson said, "you draw their fire and skip away. I'll be setting up for a clear shot. If I'm close enough, I may not even have to risk a shot." He patted the sheath of his KA-BAR knife with its seven-inch blade.

"Let's rock and roll."

"We'd better take along all of their extra ammo we can carry. I expect we'll need it."

Garson loaded his backpack with some of the ammo and slipped it on.

They pulled on night-vision goggles over their masks.

Lee whispered, "Now we're ready."

"They're waiting for us," Garson whispered back. "Let's not disappoint."

They both turned and headed off into the woods, accompanied by steady and growing thunder. Neither of them made a sound.

Chapter Twenty-Five

The last of the trooper cars' lights and those of the ranch were finally out of sight behind their speeding car. Al had been watching
the sky beyond the range of the headlights grow even darker. When
he'd been outside talking with Sidney, he'd noticed he couldn't see any
stars or the moon.

A giant bolt of white light slashed down practically onto the road
ahead of them. The thunder sounded like a huge ripping boom that rattled the vehicle.

"What the hell was that?" Maury said from the back seat.

"Lightning," Al said. "The sky is covered with clouds. First time in
months."

As if to confirm his statement, rain pounded down on the car, hard
at first, then climbing up a notch to a blinding, smashing downpour.

Al switched on his high beams and slowed. He could barely see a
dozen feet ahead. He could see no vehicles behind him nor any oncom-
ing traffic. But he couldn't go as quickly as he wanted to. He could barely see at all.

They plodded along, engulfed by the sound of hammering rain and
wipers going at full blast.

"Doesn't rain all summer, and then 'boom.' It sure makes up for it,"
Fergie said.

Al finally spotted an overpass ahead. Good. He had been remem-
bering it and hoping he didn't pass it in the blinding downpour.

He slowed and pulled over, all the way to the right, out of the lanes
of traffic. He turned off the lights so some blinded tomfool coming up

the road behind them wouldn't smash into their back end after thinking they marked a lane of traffic.

As soon as they'd moved under the overpass, the sound changed. They could still hear the rain, but the inside of the car seemed as still as doom.

"I don't know when I've been more scared in my life," Maury said.

"It's just rain." Al glanced at Maury in the rearview mirror, seeing him dimly.

"I meant back there at Luther's ranch. I was almost certain he was going to have those two big thugs kill me and bury me off somewhere I'd never be found."

"What kept him from it?" Fergie asked.

"I think he was just waiting to see if I was missed or if anyone knew where I was at."

"Well, you were missed," Al said. "We're glad to have you back."

"Oh. I've got to talk to Bonnie. But they kept my phone."

"Here. Use this one." Fergie took hers out of her pocket and handed it back to him. "Just speed-dial the B listing."

"I'm trying," he said, "but I'm getting no answer. Why would she turn her phone off?" He handed the phone back up to Fergie.

"Let's hope it's some harmless reason," Al said.

"I don't know. Maybe we'd better keep moving, and pronto," Fergie said.

Al sighed. He flipped on the lights and pulled back onto the road and headed out from under the overpass into the deluge. Water was up over the road in spots, enough that he could hydroplane if he wasn't watching it. What good news he could glean from looking around was that at least he could see no vehicle lights in any direction. Saner folk must have taken cover and stayed there.

He stepped on the gas and risked some slipping and sliding moments. Still, the road conditions forced him to slow through several stretches.

Maury seemed restless for a stretch of road, perhaps concerned or worried. Then, after a spell of awkward silence, he spoke.

"For the first time, I started to realize why you guys do what you do," Maury said from the back seat.

Al kept his eyes on the road, doing all he could to keep them from hydroplaning and slipping right off the road. Weeks of no rain and extreme heat had baked the ground so much that the rain couldn't soak into the ground. Puddles stretched across the already slippery road, hubcap deep in places and climbing.

"It's because it feels so good when you do get to go home. I suppose a real appreciation of life depends on being tested. Right?"

Al let Maury talk on. If it calmed him, great.

"I mean, life has to matter. You have to stop more to savor. Enjoy. Love. Engage."

Al glanced at Fergie. Her eyes showed she was feeling every slide and fishtail as Al drove uncomfortably fast.

"Think about those people in the past who just got by," Maury said. "Islanders, natives, aborigines. People who merely watched their lives pass by. We have so much more."

Al came close to telling Maury to put a sock in it, but at least he was calm, while he could feel Fergie's palpable tension and his own.

On the next curve, the car slid in gravel as one wheel touched the shoulder. The steering wheel jerked beneath Al's hands as he forced the car back onto the road, its back wheels fishtailing in grass for a moment.

Once back on the asphalt, he took a deep breath and slowed the car down. *No sense in not getting there at all.*

He caught a glimpse of Maury's face in the rearview mirror. The parts that hadn't taken on a blush from Cynthia's slaps had turned an ashen hue. His eyes were open wider.

"It's sure taking a long time to get there. I would have rather you went to make sure Bonnie was safe first."

"Her we knew about. You were the one missing in action. Besides, we're just about there."

"Just about. Just about." Maury's record got stuck on that.

"You know, I was driving the truck around and noticed that my registration sticker on the windshield had expired almost three months before," Al said.

Fergie gave him a sideways glance.

"I pulled in at the inspection place nearest us, and there was no line. One guy sat on a bench outside the garage door, staring off at nothing. I explained I'd let the sticker expire and needed to get caught up. As he got slowly to his feet, I said, 'The years sure go faster.' He looked at me with beagle-sad eyes and said, 'But the days go slower.'"

After a short pause, Maury asked, "Which do you think is right?"

"They both are. That's the point, after all," Al said.

Maury was silent and Fergie too for the next couple of miles. Al could just hear the whirl and splashing of the tires gripping the road and clawing through puddles and wet stretches. Rain beat down hard on the car's roof.

Al was trying to work out how many miles they had to go yet and if they had enough gas. The ground that had been dry for months around the road was meanwhile routing the accumulating water onto the road in more spots, forcing him to slow to a near crawl to get across some stretches that might send them shooting off the road. He'd been to many the scene of a fatality where the hubris of a driver had battled rising waters, and the waters had won. Once, two teenaged boys had thought their Jeep could do anything. Rescue workers found the jeep on its side a half dozen miles down the swollen stream. One boy's body they found in a tree. They never found the other boy.

A long slow stretch of tense driving gave Al the sense of taffy being stretched, his nerves along with it. The other two in the car were just as twitchy.

Finally, Fergie said, "There's something you're trying to decide, isn't there?"

"Why do you say that?"

"Admit it."

He smiled to himself.

"Ah," Fergie said. "You've already made up your mind, haven't you?"

"Maybe."

"Well, maybe I'm pleased about that."

"We'll see how that holds up," Al said. "Stands the test of time."

She looked out her window, humming to herself.

From the back seat, Maury asked, "Whatever in the hell are you two talking about?"

Chapter Twenty-Six

Bonnie was holding the baby on the couch, just wiping Little Al's face with a cloth after breastfeeding him. Tanner sat curled up beside them on the couch. He got up, walked over to the door, and stood on four stiff legs as he growled.

"Uh oh," Bonnie said.

She went into the bedroom, put the baby down, and took out sturdy clothes. The jeans were a struggle. She might have gained a pound or two of baby weight, but Maury liked her that way, called her his muffin. He'd changed the most of all of them—a former horndog who belatedly became a loving husband and father. *Who knew?* Al and Fergie were changing too, in their own ways and at their own pace.

She took a deep breath and fastened the jeans. A dark-blue shirt might be best, she thought. The ninjas love blue. She was trying to keep her thoughts light and playful to offset the raw fear growing like a knot inside her.

She shoved her stubby Smith & Wesson into her left jeans pocket. It felt too snug there. So she squeezed it inside the front of the jeans, finding a spot that still allowed her to move around. All she needed was a knife in one hand and a parrot on her shoulder, and she would feel like a pirate. Kidding herself wasn't working as much as she would've liked. She was near tears as she got out Little Al's papoose baby carrier. She slipped him into it. He was too sated from his meal to fuss much. Then she went looking for Tanner's leash.

Flipping on a few extra lights in the trailer, she left the area by the front door dark outside. She opened the door a crack, peeked around, then slipped outside into the bathwater-warm air. Locking the door behind her, so as not to make getting inside too easy, she led Tanner down the stairs, shushing his growling.

The space beneath the trailer was partially screened by a white wooden lattice. She had to tug Tanner along. He strained at the leash to go out into the dark after whatever he'd been smelling.

She squeezed in under the trailer, knowing Maury would get a chuckle out of seeing how difficult it was. Once under there, she turned around and, holding her baby with one hand and Tanner close with the other, she peered out at the expanse of dark outside the dim glow coming from the trailer's windows.

A sudden crack and boom accompanied a bolt of lightning that hit the ground less than fifty yards away and shook the dirt beneath her while lighting up the whole area.

In the brief flash of white light, she saw someone bent low scurrying her way, and she thought she could make out a weapon, a rifle of some kind. She put a hand over Tanner's muzzle, suppressing the low rumble of his growl.

Footsteps pounding up to the trailer made her heart stop. She had to hold Tanner, who struggled to attack and defend their home. His legs churned. He tried to growl, and she fought to keep him from doing so. Whoever was on the stairs pounded at the door.

Bonnie had way too much to do for someone with only two hands. She wanted to get out a gun. She wanted to dig her cell phone out of her back pocket. But she also had to keep one hand over the baby's mouth to keep it from crying out, and the other hand held Tanner's mouth closed so he wouldn't bark, though he was growling low.

The guy on the steps could have probably bashed in the front door if he had a battering ram or something, she figured. Instead, he ran back down the stairs, stood a short distance from the trailer, and opened fire.

Bam. Bam. Bam. Bam. Bam. Bam. Bam!

Shots slammed into the trailer above her. She heard glass shattering inside and splinters flying out from wood over the thumping sound of bullets pounding through the trailer's metal sides.

The shooting stopped for a second. Bonnie realized her eyes were tightly closed. She opened them. The space in front of the trailer was empty. The camo-wearing person shooting was gone. Then she heard a crackle. Something was on fire. In a couple more ticks, she saw dancing light growing in a reflection on the few surrounding trees she could see. Something in the trailer was on fire, and she was under it.

Tanner growled more loudly, and Little Al was trying hard to cry under her pressing hand. Bonnie wanted to scream herself. She saw the first flames leap up from the dry grass and bushes around the trailer. They'd caught too, and now a grass fire had begun.

She could see more clearly. Another bolt of lightning shot down so close that the clap of thunder was almost instantaneous. It lit up the entire area, enough for her to see someone wearing black stand up a good thirty feet away from the trailer.

Holy mackaroonies! There are more.

While the area was lit in the flash of light, she saw the figure in black drop back to the ground, disappearing like some jack-in-the-box.

She had no idea what was going on, and it was all happening so quickly that everything seemed to swirl. Above her, she could hear the trailer burning in earnest now, its yellow glow lighting up the area around the trailer, which was now also mostly on fire.

As if that wasn't enough, the guy in camo popped out of wherever he'd been hiding and opened fire on the trailer again in fully automatic strings of shots that raked back and forth across the side of the trailer.

She realized her face was wet with tears that were as much from helpless anger as fear. But she didn't dare let go of her baby's mouth or Tanner's muzzle, or they were all goners.

Bolts of lightning struck down one after the other. *Boom. Boom. Boom!* Thunder rolled in a continuous wave.

Then it began to rain.

The first drops came in a sudden rush that swelled almost at once into a furious downpour. The sound of drops hammering onto the trailer were as loud as a marching band going back and forth across the metal roof. Mud splashed up in sprays from the once very dry, dusty ground. Streams and pools formed.

The absolute deluge put out some of the fires in the grass. Where wood had caught, embers glittered on, sizzling in the rain.

She could hear fires still burning in the trailer above her, but the rain seemed to muffle some of that noise.

Yet it didn't stop that idiot with the gun. He continued to spray round after round into the trailer.

Bonnie didn't know if the trailer contained a tank of fuel that could explode but suspected it did. She couldn't stay here forever.

Outside the edge of what was left of the awning, rain came down in an absolute downpour, a real frog-walloper. She was glad for the noise. It was all she could do to keep from screaming as the pounding rain and firing bullets continued.

Finally, she had to risk it. She took her hand off Tanner's mouth. He didn't bark, bless him, though he growled more loudly. She hoped the rain and shooting would cover the noise.

She struggled to get the phone out of her pocket while still holding onto Little Al's mouth. Of course the damn thing was slippery as a bar of soap this once. She dropped it twice before she could speed-dial Fergie's number.

When Fergie answered, she said, "You gotta help me! They're coming at us. But get here as quick—"

Footsteps hammered up the steps to the trailer again, and this time the camo guy must have pointed his gun right at the door's lock. He fired at least two dozen rounds right at it. Then she heard him yank the door open so that he could see inside.

She didn't know how long he would take inside before coming back down the stairs and maybe looking under the trailer.

Bonnie jammed the phone back into a pocket and put one hand on the butt of her Chief's Special, still shoved inside her belt. She clenched the checked wooden grip tightly in her fist and lay trembling under the trailer, expecting to see a face look under it at any moment.

Chapter Twenty-Seven

Fergie's phone rang. Al watched her glance at the caller ID.

"Hmm. It's Bonnie." She flipped on the speaker phone and answered.

"You gotta help me! They're coming at us. But get here as quick—"

That was it. The call stopped abruptly.

Al thought he had heard gunfire in the background.

"What's going on?" Maury's voice went up an octave.

"I'm trying to call her back, but she's not answering," Fergie said.

The rain hadn't let up the least bit. Lightning was striking every few seconds in all directions around them, and the thunder was a steady rolling roar that rose and fell but didn't let up at all.

Al pressed on the gas pedal, putting it almost to the floor. If some cop tried to stop them, they'd just have to deal with it.

The Civic's engine roared as best it could, straining but surging all the same. It handled better than Al could have hoped.

He let up only going into curves, accelerating as soon as he was into them to shoot through to the next open stretch. He was thankful for straight stretches since he could still see barely fifteen feet ahead.

He tried to figure how many miles he had to go. *Too many.* Especially if Bonnie was already in trouble.

"The baby," Maury said. "And Bonnie, of course."

Al included Tanner. He hoped the dog was okay too.

"We can be there in five or ten minutes," Fergie said. "Should you call the sheriff's department and let them know?"

"Let them know what? We don't even know what's going on," Al said. "Let's just get there and see first. You know the procedure, Fergie.

We've got to have visual confirmation before we willy-nilly ask the department to pull out the stops. We're only a few moments away."

"Well, just get there then," she said.

Al rushed through the turns, sliding a bit, throwing gravel now and then, but neither Fergie nor Maury complained.

As he came at last to the turn into the drive that led to the trailer, he went right past it.

"What are you doing?" Maury shouted from the back seat, his voice still in an upper register.

"He's getting us into position to come in from a direction where we're not expected," Fergie said.

"Oh."

Al saw a likely place ahead, far enough away yet close enough that they could hike there quickly. As he pulled in, he spotted a silver Subaru tucked up close to the trunk of a thick tree that had to be hundreds of years old. He hit the brakes.

"Fergie," was all he said.

He opened his door, popped the trunk, and shot around toward it. As soon as he was out of the car, rain plastered his hair to his forehead and soaked through everything he was wearing, making him cold and damp all the way to his underwear. After the past few days of baking heat and drought, it didn't feel as bad as it might have.

He was breathing more easily as he reached inside the trunk. If anyone was lurking close around them, he'd have already been shot or at least shot at. But he didn't slow. He opened the canvas bag and took out the weapons and the Taser. Then he zipped the bag back up.

Putting his Sig Sauer at his back, he grabbed the sawed-off and took off in a crouch for the Subaru. He peeked inside, ready to fire. But it was empty except for a baby seat. Stolen, probably. He would call it in later.

He could hear shooting in the distance. Lots and lots of it. He hoped they weren't too late.

Fergie was standing by the trunk when he came back to their Civic. Her eyes carried the same urgent concern he was feeling. She held the Ruger in one hand.

Maury stood on one foot then the other. "Hurry. Hurry. We have to hurry."

Al rushed to the Honda's glove box and looked inside. His hopes rose when he found a red plastic flashlight then faded as he flipped it on. All he could get from it was a dim brownish-yellow circle. The batteries were borderline shot. But it was better than nothing.

He rushed to the back of the car. He handed the sawed-off shotgun and the PPK to Maury.

"Your job is to get Bonnie and the baby out of there, as fast as you can."

"What about this?" Still holding the Ruger in one hand, Fergie picked up the only remaining weapon, the Taser.

"Maury can carry the Taser too." Al closed the trunk and locked the Civic, though that might not matter an iota before all this was over.

"What good will that do?" Maury asked.

"If you get scared, you can Tase yourself." Al didn't wait for a response. He handed the flashlight to Fergie and took off at a near run toward where he could hear at least one, maybe two automatic weapons firing away.

As he ran, he tugged out his phone and punched in Clayton's personal number. As soon as Clayton answered, Al shouted, "You'd better get SWAT out to your trailer. All hell's breaking loose there! There's a stolen Subaru here too, but that's the least of your worries, considering who probably stole it." He hung up and kept running.

Chapter Twenty-Eight

Tanner struggled to get free of Bonnie's grasp to go out and grab the leg of the guy unloading yet another clip into the trailer. The shooter had to know the trailer was empty. Bonnie knew the guy would gun down a dog without hesitation. The thunder and pounding rain, as well as the crackle of a fire still going on just above her head, made enough noise to cover Tanner's steady growling.

At least Little Al had cried himself out for a spell and was working hard on a binky. His eyes were open wide.

Bonnie worked her Chief's Special loose from behind her belt with an effort that took more twisting and turning than she expected. She made a note to herself to never practice quick draw beneath a trailer while holding onto a dog and a baby, in a thunderstorm, with a fire going on in the trailer and a guy still shooting at it.

By the time she had the gun clear, the guy had disappeared. She knew why in a second. The light from the burning trailer lit up enough of the area around for her to see a guy in black stand up again from behind a stand of cactus, one of the only areas not smoldering from the fire that had swept through, now just flickers of red embers sizzling as drops of rain plopped onto them.

The guy in black stood there a moment, looking around, then someone wearing camo leaped up from the ground beside him. The flash of a silver knife blade went to the neck of the guy in black, and he was pulled to the ground, out of sight.

"Well, blast it. I've got six bullets here and no one to shoot." Bonnie would have been hard pressed to explain whether she was talking to Tanner or Little Al. She did know she had to get out from under this trailer before it blew up, or whatever burning trailers do. She could feel the heat emanating from it.

She peered out into the dimly lit area around her, the rain forming a silver curtain that cleared for seconds, only to become an impenetrable blur again. If she had been alone, she would have pulled herself out from under there and tried to scamper away. But she didn't want to take the risk with Little Al and Tanner.

Now, all she could do was stay hunkered and hope they didn't all get blown to kingdom come anyway. The rain drummed down, the fire in the trailer crackled, and she couldn't tell if she was crying or if the wetness on her cheeks was from the rain.

JIM PERKINS HAD CRAWLED close enough to see the guy in camo spraying the trailer from one end to the other, punching bullet holes waist high then spraying shots in a crisscross pattern back and forth that would have taken out anyone inside.

He lifted his H&K and lined up the sights on the guy. His slow squeeze on the trigger was interrupted by two things. The shooter suddenly darted away, just disappearing. The other thing was that someone grabbed him. He saw the silver edge of a KA-BAR blade against his neck, and whoever had him dragged him to the ground.

He struggled to look behind him, but the only glimpse he got was of two piercing eyes behind a black ski mask. For a second, he thought the worst. *This is the last thing I'm ever going to see, isn't it?*

GARSON HAD SEEN THE black form low on the ground, probably thinking he was invisible. He wasn't. Night-vision goggles usually need some scrap of light, what they can get from the moon or stars. None of that was available in this cloud-covered downpour. But the light from the burning trailer gave him what he needed. He knew not to look directly at the fire, or he'd not be able to see a thing for a spell. The goggles would grab and magnify the flames.

As he got closer, he took off the goggles and slipped them into his backpack. Only a few steps more.

Lee stepped out into the open again in front of the trailer. He unloaded another clip into it. As expected, the agent in black stood up and aimed his H&K. Garson had slithered close enough. He rose from the ground and knocked the gun out of the agent's hands. In a second, he stood behind him, knife at the agent's throat. He could feel the thickness of the bulletproof vest the agent wore, but that wasn't going to do him any good at the moment.

"Please. Please. Please."

Garson couldn't tell if that meant "please make it quick," or "please don't kill me."

He surprised the agent, and himself, by coming down on the guy's temple with the butt of his KA-BAR.

The guy collapsed and lay there in the rain.

Garson found cuffs, two pair, and used them to cuff one wrist to the opposing ankle, then the other two limbs the same way, turning the agent into a pretzel. If this guy managed to move, it was going to be something to behold.

He wasn't sure why he hadn't killed the agent or how he'd explain it to Lee. Maybe he wouldn't say anything.

Garson took all the ammo he could find, along with the H&K, of course. Now he had some serious firepower.

Instead of taking off right away, Garson squatted there in the hammering rain, as if its wet chill could affect the furnace inside him. The FBI guy lay there as out of it as mod clothes, Nehru jackets, and Beatle boots. Garson wondered again if he should tell E. J. that he hadn't killed the agent. *Ah well.* Maybe he hadn't seen much, what with the mask. Though guys like this were apt to take it personal and come after a target all the harder. Garson was just tired, tired of it all.

When he was like this, he could see Ginger's face, not the pretty one, but the angry one. Like she had a lot to be mad about. Still and all...

For some reason, he drifted to thinking about a time late in his teens when he'd been friendly with a married woman in her thirties. She'd sure taught him a lot. She wasn't so much married as separated, and the things she knew...

They'd been lying there in bed one evening, giving him time to rest for twenty minutes so they could go again. *Man, I was sure a machine in those days.* Then he heard the front door open and close downstairs.

"Who's that?"

"It's probably Roger," she said.

"The husband?"

"Yeah."

Garson knew the guy, a lunk of a fellow with tattoos and knuckled fists like bricks.

"You'd better make yourself scarce."

Scarce? There was only one of him. Garson looked around. He leaped up and was tugging on his clothes as footsteps pounded up the stairway, coming their way.

He was out the open window just as the bedroom door opened.

"What are you doing naked?"

"Waiting on you, baby."

He could hear every word clearly because he was hanging by his fingers from the outside sill of the window. He looked down—quite a ways down from the second story.

"What the hell you got that window open for?"

"You know how hot I get."

Garson let go and dropped to the ground with a thump, twisting one ankle. He took off in a hobbling run and was around the corner of the house before the guy's stupid head could lean out and look around. The dog was just coming out of its house. He whizzed past that and was over the fence before the dog got there, but just barely. It growled and barked on the other side.

Maybe his ankle hurting the way it did now had made him think of that. *Who knew?* Maybe Ginger had a point about his taking the whole thing with the senator too personally. But he'd once been on the other side of that, for what it was worth.

Well, stewing over that wasn't going to fix anything. He needed to find Lee and see if the job of taking out the witnesses was already over or not.

He looked up into the rain, letting it soak the ski mask and his face. He wanted to get clear of here. The fire in the trailer still glowed but was dimmer. The rain was doing what it could to put that out. He would circle around that way and see if he could locate Lee. They'd looked at some walkie-talkies at the surplus store but decided they worked better in the quiet. But they hadn't foreseen every detail of a night like this one was turning out to be.

Chapter Twenty-Nine

Lee sat on his haunches in a blackened spot of ground where the fire had already swept past. He'd put the night-vision goggles back on. Now, he waited. He figured Garson had already taken out one of those Bu guys. But the other was still out there and hadn't shown himself.

He swept the area all around, scanning for any movement. Flickers of embers, still alive, showed here and there, some of them sputtering out in the deluge that hammered him.

It was a shame he'd found no one in the trailer. That would have really simplified everything. He'd hoped to be done with this whole mess, maybe already be in Mexico, knocking back shots of tequila and trying to learn the language. He knew *basta* and half a dozen other words. But he expected to have plenty of time to pick up the rest.

Then, though he struggled against it, he began to think of Brenda. He tried to recall the excitement of first meeting her, the magic of their first months together. The wedding, truth be told, was more for her than him, but he'd truly loved her. *Where the hell did all that go wrong?* Her succumbing to the advances of that asshole Bentley. Well, that had been only the first step of the downhill slide.

He'd never cheated on her, other than the usual chance mingling with whores when on R&R. *But what the hell? I was overseas.*

Well, it did little good to think of all that now. He had this one little chore to do, and he would be out of here and not looking back.

To hell with Brenda. To hell with everything!

AL, FERGIE, AND MAURY were still three or four hundred yards from the trailer. Their steps splashed loudly in the shallow pools of water through which they waded. Al no longer worried about the noise, lost in the din of the pouring rain. He could barely see anything around them in the slanted silver lines of rain. He stayed close to Fergie, who suddenly stopped.

She was in the lead with the flashlight, which was getting dimmer by the minute. "What the bloody hell is that?"

Al and Maury crowded close, looking ahead to where her beam pointed. Fergie's light was fixed on what looked like a chupacabra to Al. It looked just like the one in Flora-Ida's photo, only this one was alive with glittering eyes and drool coming from its mouth. The thing about coyotes is they are essentially cowards. They don't want to be near people, and they scoot. They are more comfortable around calves and fawns. This thing just stood there, staring at them. Then it broke into a run, coming right at them. Al had never heard of a coyote attacking a human, especially three of them. Yet here it came at full gallop.

Fergie gave a short scream. Maury pointed the sawed-off he held and squeezed one of the triggers.

Boom!

The grey blur slid to a stop and turned to take off in the opposite direction at a full run.

"Did I kill it?" Maury asked.

"I doubt you did more than sting it a bit at this distance. You've got to realize that a gun with a barrel as short as the one you're holding is going to spray a pretty wide pattern from this far away. Save your other barrel until we're closer... to anything."

"What the hell was that?" Fergie said. "I thought those things didn't really exist."

"Me either," Al said. "but I'd hate to have to answer a lie detector just now about what I think I saw."

"Bonnie and Little Al," Maury said. "I wonder if—"

"Don't get ahead of yourself. They're probably fine." *Or have worse things to worry about.*

The automatic weapon that had been firing away had stopped. That was by no means a good sign.

"We'd better get moving, and pronto," he said.

"You'll get no argument from me," Fergie said.

They all crowded closer to her and her fading light as they moved more quickly through the pouring rain.

E. J. PUNCHED THE NUMBER and waited. Nothing. He gave it a while then punched it in again. They'd agreed to set their cell phones on vibrate and only use them if they absolutely had to, in an emergency. But he hadn't heard or seen Jim in too long. *Why isn't he answering?* He put the phone away and looked around.

The shooting had stopped, and now all he heard was the relentless sound of rain. Then he heard a boom in the distance. Someone had fired a shotgun, and neither he nor Jim had one.

He'd waited long enough, maybe too long. He tucked his H&K under one arm and pulled out his cell phone. Lifting it up, he caught a grey blur from the corner of his eye. Then something slammed into him as hard as a football linebacker on a blitz.

His H&K fell out from under his arm, and his cell phone flew off into the night, landing somewhere in the puddles spreading over most of the hard, sun-baked ground.

Whatever had him knocked him to the ground. Its teeth were locked onto his chest, sunk deep into his bulletproof vest.

He hit at the furry thing with his fists. Its head shook from side to side as it sought to tear a chunk of him free. He couldn't even get to his sidearm. His hands were too busy, one arm covering his neck to keep the thing from going for his throat. With the other hand, he tried to push the crazed thing from him so that he could stand up.

He'd never in his life been so close to something that seemed so full of raw fury.

"OH MY GOD. THERE IT is again." Fergie stopped.

Al thought they weren't far from the trailer. But when he looked ahead, he saw the grey shape again. It was on top of someone, snarling and shaking its head. Its teeth were locked on the black form, which struggled beneath it.

"Now?" Maury said.

"Might as well," Al said. They were too far away to do much good with the scatter gun, but it had made the animal move before.

Boom!

As soon as Maury fired the other barrel, he started digging in his pocket for the extra shells Al had suggested he bring along.

Al stepped around to the front, in case the beast turned and charged them. But it rose off the man it had been holding to the ground and took off in a loping and only slightly limping run.

The man got up, scrambling awkwardly to his feet, and took off running in another direction.

"Should we go after him?" Fergie asked.

"I don't think that's one of the ones we have to worry about." He'd caught a brief flicker of the large white letters that said FBI on the flak jacket. He thought there was a good chance Maury had winged the agent some with his buckshot blast, so he didn't fancy a chat with the guy at the moment. "We're not that far from the trailer. Let's go there."

Maury closed the shotgun on two fresh shells. "Yeah. Let's."

Al felt a surge of quiet pride in his brother. There had been a day, just a year or two back, when he'd never fired a gun and certainly was far from calm under any kind of battle pressure. But here he was, blasting away at chupacabras and federal agents. *Good for him.* If they got through all this in one piece, Al might just tell him so.

Chapter Thirty

E.J. was still running when he finally got all the way back to the Bureau SUV. He stopped, panting, and listened for the sound of anyone or anything that might be following him.

Just the steady sound of rain, less of a deluge now, but still coming down. The ground was done soaking up what it could and was forming small ponds and rivulets through the brownish scrub and open patches around him.

Time to call for backup. He reached for his cell phone. It wasn't there. He'd left his H&K back there too. He thought he could hear the first threads of sirens in the far distance.

He opened the SUV and slid inside. He turned on the interior lights and looked at his face in the rearview mirror. Just as he thought. He looked like a kid with acne. Tiny shotgun pellet holes dotted his face. The dots stung. Some were starting to redden. He was just damned lucky none had caught him in the eye.

His left arm hurt too. He pulled up his sleeve. Yep. Whatever had been chewing on him had caught him with its toothy jaws there too. The front of his bulletproof vest was chewed into a frayed mess. That was the luckiest bit of all, or he'd be a gutted corpse back there.

He sat and thought a moment. He should go back there and see what happened to Jim. That would be the right thing to do. But he was shaking. He didn't want to go back.

His sidearm was still in its holster. He checked the glove box and took out a small first-aid kit and a heavy-duty four-cell flashlight. He put the flashlight on the seat beside himself and took out some gauze to clean the wound on his arm.

Yeah, he should get back there, but he figured he had a right to patch himself up first. He listened for the threads of sirens he'd heard, hoping they would get louder and closer. But they still seemed a long way off. He put some disinfectant on the raw, open gash of his arm wound, added some gauze, and taped it up.

Give it a few minutes, he figured. Jim was probably tromping this direction even as he sat there.

He could still see the hideous thing as it had slavered over him, clawing and chewing at his vest. In the dark, he couldn't tell if it had been foaming at the mouth, but that's the way he imagined it, how it replayed in his head.

E. J. realized he was shaking, hard and uncontrollably. He tried to will himself against it, but it was bigger than he was. He supposed he was going to have to get a damn rabies shot now too.

Maybe if he ran the engine, took out some of the growing chill from the SUV's interior. He put the key in the ignition and turned it. Nothing. *What the hell?*

He tried again. Still nothing. *They couldn't have.* But he popped the hood with the interior release, took the long-handled flashlight, and went out into the rain to have a look.

Inside, where the distributor cap should be, he saw nothing.

Now, he had to think like one of them. He started in circles that widened and got farther each time. He didn't imagine they'd gone far with the damned thing.

Finally, after twenty minutes in the pouring wet, he spotted a pile of loose brush and leaf litter at the base of a tree. He brushed away the loose cover, and there it was.

He dug out the distributor cap from the loose dirt and mud, brushing it off. He carried it back to the SUV.

Of course, the spark-plug wires took longer than usual to find and reattach. At last, he had it back the way it had been. He closed the hood, slogged back to the driver's side, and slid his wet butt in.

This time, the engine started. He reached and turned on the heater.

Ah. He would just sit here and wait. He was wounded, after all. Then he started thinking about guys able to gain entry to an FBI SUV and remove its distributor cap. How did they know where to go to find the witnesses? Oh, man. The answer was simple and obvious. He hated to do it, but he took the flashlight and opened his door and stepped back into the rain. He went around to the back of the vehicle because that's how he would've done it. He plopped down in the slick mud and pools of water, leaned back until he was horizontal, and pushed with his heels, slipping a bit in the mud, until he was beneath the back end of the SUV. He flashed the light around. *There it is.* A GPS tracker. It looked like the kind you could buy at any spyware store, cheap but effective. He wrenched it loose and slid back out. He got to his feet and let the rain rinse away some of the mud from his back. He took a few steps away from the vehicle and tried to hurl the damn thing into the woods, but his arm was too sore. He settled for underhanding it as far away as he could. He sure as hell would leave that out of any report.

He got back inside and let the air from the heater wash over him, wishing he had some kind of towel. No such luck, so he just rubbed at his sore arm, which was beginning to tingle. Then he sat and wondered what the devil had happened to Jim.

FERGIE APPROACHED THE trailer first since she had the light, one that was nearly spent. Al and Maury were following close behind. But Maury surged into a run as Bonnie began to climb out from under the trailer. She let go of the leash, and Tanner rushed to Al, who went to a knee to give the dog a hug and get a few licks.

Maury and Bonnie hugged as if they'd been apart for years. Maybe it seemed that way. Al could understand. The last couple or three days seemed to have stacked a year or two's worth of experiences into a very short period of time.

"We've got to get clear of this damn trailer," he said.

"Yeah. You're lucky the thing didn't blow up on you," Fergie said.

"It still could." Al took Tanner's leash.

Bonnie and Maury held hands as they scurried behind Al and Fergie. Enough of a fire, even though most of it had been doused by the rain, still burned inside the trailer, giving them light to slink off into the closest thick patch of burnt tree trunks and diminished shrubs.

Al paused. He looked around and listened. When he couldn't detect anyone near, he stepped close, and they all gathered in a huddle.

"Maury, if something starts to happen, and there's a good chance it will, I want you to scoot for where we left the Civic. Okay?"

Maury nodded.

"You'd better give the PPK to Bonnie. She's a far better shot than you," Fergie said.

"Really? You were heeled?" Bonnie tilted her head at Maury.

"And soled." He took out the pistol and handed it to her.

"I forgot I still had it," Maury said.

"If you have to use the shotgun again, wait until they're closer, Maury. You're just stinging them and pissing them off from a distance."

"It worked getting rid of that…" He hesitated, glancing toward Bonnie. "Whatever it was."

"Should I ask?" Bonnie said.

"Might be better if you didn't." Maury reached to cup Little Al's face.

The baby was asleep, his binky threatening to fall out of his mouth. Then he sucked it tighter and closer.

"That's the boy. He can sleep through just about anything."

"I wonder where he gets that?" Bonnie said.

"Listen," Al said. "We have to go. Now." He grasped Maury's hand and slipped him the keys to the Civic as he did.

He could hear distant sirens, low enough to be still a few miles away.

"Couldn't we just wait and hope for help to arrive?" Maury asked.

"I wish we could, but no." Al turned and started off in the direction of the Civic.

Fergie eased into the front with her frail, flickering, dim light.

Chapter Thirty-One

L ee didn't like this. He didn't like it at all. The ground felt slick with a soupy wet he had to slosh through with every step. The rain was coming down in a steady pour, cutting visibility to ten or fifteen feet. *Nothing says your time is running out like a bunch of sirens coming your way and getting closer every second.* He moved more quickly through the wasteland the fire had made. Far fewer shrubs and almost no grass were there, but visibility through the rain was nowhere near perfect.

He needed to find Garson and get out of here. An FBI agent was still around here too. He'd seen Garson take one of them down—probably cut his throat.

They'd failed in their objective. *Had that just been a trap by those FBI guys?* He hadn't gotten any sign of the witnesses they were looking for.

He looped out and around, seeking the spot where he'd last seen Garson. *No sign of him this time, and forget about looking for any foot-prints.*

Then he saw a wavering flicker of light ahead coming his way. He crouched lower and eased behind the blackened bottom of a tree trunk.

FERGIE WAS GETTING a little ahead of them. Al wanted to call out but didn't dare yell.

Behind him, he heard a splash. When he looked back, Bonnie was lying on her back in a puddle with her arms and legs flailing.

Maury rushed to her, bent first to check the baby, then tried to pull Bonnie to her feet by grabbing her arms. She slipped out of his grasp and flipped to her side, careful not to roll onto Little Al.

"You'd better give me a hand," Maury whispered as loud as he could.

Al looked ahead. Fergie was getting away from them. He rushed back and put his arms under Bonnie's armpits and hoisted her upright.

"I'm okay. I'm okay," she kept saying.

Maury brushed at her, trying to get some of the mud off. The steady rain was helping some.

"Let's go. Let's go," Al said. "We need to catch up with Fergie."

Tanner growled, low at first, then growing louder.

Al turned and saw her, barely able to make her out in the distance through the rain. But what he did see chilled him far more than the wet cold, which went all the way to his underwear. Someone wearing camo was standing behind Fergie and had the blade of a knife held up to her neck.

Al spun to Maury and Bonnie. "You two, go out and around. Move as fast as you can and stay as far away as you can. We'll meet up back where we left the Civic."

"But—" Maury started to say.

"Do it. Just go. This may be the only way to save Bonnie and the baby. Just get to the car."

"But I can hear those sirens getting louder."

"I wish that mattered more than it does just now."

Maury and Bonnie took off to the right, seeking to go far out and away from the situation ahead.

Al dropped to the ground. He tied Tanner's leash to the singed foot-high stump of a mesquite tree and slithered ahead through the mud and wet black ash. He rubbed some on his face to become even less visible.

When he got within twenty feet, the guy yelled out, "I see you there, slithering along like a snake! That isn't going to matter a whit if I have to cut your lady friend."

"What do you want?" Al yelled. He slid forward a few more feet, daring to close the distance since the guy wasn't pointing a gun at him, though Al could see he had one slung over his shoulder that would probably be pretty easy to get to. Al was close enough now to make out the camo clothes and the black ski mask.

"You were the ones there at Bentley's place, weren't you?" the guy yelled.

Al slid forward another foot or two.

"We didn't see your faces, though. Still haven't seen them. We'd be worthless in a court of law."

"That doesn't matter now. Very little matters now except you guys gotta go. Sorry and all that." The guy chuckled.

"Why? Are you just about killing now?"

"That seems to be the case, wouldn't you say?" The guy was close enough for Al to see him tilt his head. "Why should that bother you?"

"It gets me in the gut," Al said. "That's all."

Fergie frowned then caught on. She drove her elbow back into the guy's stomach. That should have doubled any other person over, but it only got a grunt out of this fellow. Tough stuff. He tapped Fergie on the top of her head with the butt of his knife. "Don't try that again."

He put the knife back to Fergie's throat. "Do you have any last words you'd like to share with the lady?"

From behind him, Al heard a growl that turned into a roar. A flash of grey shot past him. For a second, he thought that damned chupacabra was attacking them again. Then he saw it was Tanner. He'd pulled loose from where Al had tied him.

"No, boy. No!" Al yelled. But Tanner was a dog on a mission. "Tanner!"

The dog's leash trailed behind. Fergie was his friend too, and he was intent on saving her.

As soon as he was near, the guy in camo tried to kick him. But Tanner circled around faster than the guy expected.

Tanner leaped up and snapped at the man's left arm, which was holding Fergie in place. The guy pushed Fergie aside and to the ground. He whirled to slash at Tanner, but the strap of his AR-15 slid down his arm and slowed him enough that Tanner could leap to the side, snarling and ready to leap to the attack again.

Al used the time to leap to his feet and run as fast as he could right at the guy, who turned his head and saw Al coming a second too late.

With both hands, Al grabbed the wrist of the hand holding the knife and did a somersault in the air. His body weight did most of the work. Maybe the guy hadn't expected that of someone Al's age. Maybe he didn't even know Al's age. But his biggest surprise was the sharp crack of whatever happened to his wrist, making the knife fall from his grip.

"Al. Be careful." Fergie had seen Al in a fury of rage like this before. Even though she probably knew that he was doing it for her, that how he felt for her generated this sort of madness and energy, she sounded concerned.

The guy stood there for a second or two, his long gun falling from his lowered arm to the ground. Then he recovered and bent to reach with the other arm to grab the rifle.

Tanner rushed in, snapping his teeth. The guy kicked at him, mostly missing but connecting once in a kick that slanted off Tanner's ribs and drew a loud yip.

Whatever furnace was going inside Al only got hotter.

He charged in and swung an uppercut that hit the guy in the chin and jerked his head to one side. The blow would have felled most people, but this guy was made of tougher stuff.

Al wondered for a second if he'd broken a bone or two in his hand. But he shook the fingers and they seemed fine—sore but fine.

He kicked as hard as he could, only fair since the guy had kicked Tanner. The guy turned his hip to take the blow on his thigh, the way a well-trained mixed martial artist would.

Faster than the guy expected, Al kicked again with his left leg, a blow aimed right at the side of the guy's knee. It connected, and Al heard a loud pop and registered the surprise and jolt of pain in the eyes behind the ski mask.

He wobbled and started to crumple. Al didn't wait for him to fall but rushed in. The guy was a fighter. He lifted his arms, ready to defend. But since he could barely stand, Al rushed in, throwing punches and chops, and even got in a kick that almost took out the other knee but slid up inside the thigh and landed somewhere soft that got a grunt out of the guy.

He wasn't all defense to Al's attack. He tried to charge but stumbled. Al flew in and hit him three times in the throat. Wham. Wham. Wham. The guy fell over on top of him.

Tanner rushed in and grabbed a leg, growling and shaking his head.

Al rolled to get astride the fallen guy and smash blow after blow to the face while the guy's lifted arms grew weaker and limper.

"Al. Al. You're gonna kill the guy." Fergie tugged at his shoulder.

Al paused, reached down, and pulled off the guy's ski mask.

"Which one are you? Lee or Garson?" Al yelled.

"Lee." The name came out as a croaking gasp.

"Al, get off him."

Al stood slowly, his legs wobbly for a second. He looked around. Another one of them was still out here.

The guy on the ground coughed once then again, harder, with something stuck in his throat or his larynx damaged. He held up an arm. It flopped back to his side.

"Al?" Fergie said.

They both bent closer.

He wheezed, "Women... They're more trouble than they're worth." Lee's eyes lost their focus, and his head fell to one side.

Fergie stepped close to Al and put an arm around him. "Is that the way you feel?"

"I'm not in a position to judge about this guy's life. But I have a suspicion his opinion might be a little jaundiced."

Tanner came over to him, and Al bent to take hold of the leash. Al was still breathing hard and wouldn't care to be challenged to a race just then. But they were alive. He, Fergie, and Tanner were alive, and that was in the face of someone who didn't want them to be.

Chapter Thirty-Two

The rain was steady, and the sirens seemed to be getting closer. Bonnie could barely see, but Maury seemed to know which way to head. She stayed close to him, never happier to have someone else leading the way after what had seemed hours scrunched beneath the butt end of a trailer.

She held a hand over the baby's head, trying to shelter Little Al from the rain. With the other hand, she reached out to grasp Maury's hand. Abruptly, she tugged him closer. He turned to hug her, careful not to smoosh Little Al.

He was looking over her shoulder at the way ahead of them. She heard his "Oh crap." Then she heard the *click, click* as he pulled back both triggers of the double-barreled sawed-off he carried.

"You'd better get out one of your guns," he said.

"What?" She let go of him and spun. Without a light, all she could see ahead of them was a hulking grey form. As it limped closer, she could make out its shape then its face. "Oh my crow-eyed heavens!" With one hand, she reached up to hug Little Al closer although he was still snug in his papoose carrier. Her other hand went for the PPK tucked inside her belt.

The thing moved faster then ran, loping right toward them. Bonnie fumbled the gun out. She struggled to find the safety with one hand. The gun was unfamiliar to her, and even when she held it up to look more closely at it, she wasn't sure.

She let it drop into the mud swirling at their feet and went for her Chief's Special. She whipped it out. That she knew how to use.

The loping beast was almost to them.

"What are you waiting for?" she asked.

"It's got to get close."

"It *is* close."

"Closer," Maury said, stepping between her and the charging animal. He was calmer and steadier than she'd expected, calmer than she'd ever heard him before, and this was with a snarling beast charging right at them.

The thing was almost to them. It leaped.

Boom! Maury squeezed both barrels while the creature was in midair. It tumbled to the ground, feet going, but on its side, writhing.

Bonnie moved around Maury. She stepped close, pointed the barrel of her pistol right at the creature's head, and squeezed off two rounds. *Bam! Bam!*

She turned to Maury, her insides swelling with pride. The animal quit moving. She didn't know what it was. It didn't look quite like a coyote to her. The rain was washing some foam from its face. She looked to Maury.

He shrugged. "Chupacabra?"

"Could be. If so, it's a dead one," she said.

The baby began to cry. She tucked away her Chief's Special and bent to pick up the PPK. Maybe she'd figure out how to work it better when she had a spare moment someday. At least someday was going to come.

"I'm so proud of you, Maury, standing between your son and wife and that attacking thing."

He nodded. She thought he wanted to say something but maybe couldn't think of the exact right thing to say. Rain poured off his face.

"I'll give you my extra-special thanks when we're the heck out of here."

"Oh boy. Extra special." He could talk now.

He put a hand against her back, and they started walking again, looking around to see if the sound of the shotgun blast had attracted anyone to them.

She comforted Little Al and got him to take his binky.

Maury reached to take her hand. Bonnie moved closer and followed along. "If we weren't in the middle of a rainstorm and still in all kinds of danger," she said, "I'd throw you to the ground and have you right here."

"Whee. Mud wrestling," he said. "The car's not too far from here. Let's get moving. Who knows what kind of time we'll have when we're there?"

When they got to the car, it occurred to her that it was locked.

Maury held up the keys and jangled them. "Al slipped them to me when he sent us this way."

"I hope... I hope he and Fergie are okay. It's like him to take the heat off us."

"Yep. That's how he is, all right."

He opened the car, and she slid into the back seat with the baby. Maury slid in beside her. No baby seat, but they could get by this once.

"Please lock the doors," she said. "If Al or Fergie comes, we can let them in. No one else."

She took out her pistol and held it in one hand.

"Want to neck or something?" Maury asked.

"I just want to sit here and shiver a bit," she said. "Please hold me." So he did.

Chapter Thirty-Three

Where in the hell is he? Garson peered into the rain ahead. This had sure turned into one major screw-up. They should have set up a better communication link. He tugged his cell phone out and punched Lee's number again. *Nothing.*

He nearly threw the phone down into the swirling rivulet he was standing in. The whole damn place was a swamp, and the rain was still coming down hard enough to make visibility difficult.

Garson winced with every step. At least in this steady rain, no one could see him limping around this way. He started back toward where he'd left that agent cuffed on the ground. At least he could finish him off. Lee had probably taken care of his. It wouldn't do to leave a loose end. *What was I thinking?* Maybe he was getting soft, soft in the head.

Then he saw something moving ahead. A couple of people were coming his way. He could barely make out their shapes from where he stood. But it seemed to be a man and a woman. He and Lee were here to finish off two witnesses, possibly a man and a woman.

He reached for the strap of the H&K and pulled it off his shoulder then patted the weapon. "Looks like I'm going to get to use you after all," he whispered.

Overseas, it had always been a bad sign when one of the guys started to talk to his gun. But there were no bad signs out here on a night like this. He was about to close out their mission.

The sirens were getting damned close, but he didn't care. He was about to fulfill their reason for coming. He was cold. He was wet. His leg hurt like dammit with every step. But he was grinning. He moved forward toward the two people approaching.

FERGIE GLANCED AT HER watch. It would be morning soon, and what a night. *What a hell of a night!* She could hear the sirens coming toward them on the road. But they weren't here yet. They might as well be a million miles away, with a killer still loose in the steady rain.

She sloshed through puddles, seeking to stay as close as possible to Al this time. She could still feel the edge of that steel blade against her tender throat. She would be dreaming about that for years to come. Nightmares, really.

Tanner began to growl, low at first, then louder. Al came to a stop, and she bumped into him. He reached for her and slammed her to the ground, face-first into a puddle that felt like mostly mud. Good for the skin, probably, but she couldn't see or breathe. Then he threw himself across her, which knocked out what little air she had left.

"Umpf." She could barely wiggle an arm free to brush at her face. She needed to clear her eyes.

Tanner was growling more loudly.

Al reached to hold the dog's mouth closed. "Shhh."

As soon as Fergie was able to blink her eyes open, she could make out the guy in camo, far enough away he was lifting his weapon, close enough he wasn't likely to miss.

Al grabbed her and rolled briskly to his right.

She was reaching for the pistol in her belt, but her arms flailed, and she landed face down in the mud again with Al on top of her once more.

She struggled as gunfire broke out. *Wham. Wham. Wham. Wham.* Automatic fire sprayed right at them.

As she got her eyes clear again, she could see they were tucked behind the broad trunk of a tree.

Al lifted the AR-15 he carried and returned fire. *Bam. Bam. Bam.*

He was pacing himself, not using up what ammo he had.

The sirens were louder. Some were stopping. She wished they were right here beside them, where they could do some damned good.

She slithered out from under Al. He reached to grab her hand. "Come on. Let's go."

The camo guy must have been putting in a new clip. Heaven knew there'd been enough shots fired to use up a clip.

Al broke into a run, tugging her along until she got going. Then her long legs started to outstrip him, and she pulled ahead. He let go of her hand.

"Keep moving," he encouraged her. "This one's probably Garson."

She didn't know how it helped to know the guy's name, but she moved her feet all the same. This guy was a killer, one who'd taken out a US senator right between two Secret Service men. That was putting aside the fact that she secretly thought the senator had it coming. But she wasn't inclined to stop and congratulate this guy, especially since he was shooting at them.

Tanner still growled and gave an occasional angry bark.

Garson opened fire again, sending up sprays of mud and water as the bullets ripped along in a line toward them.

Al surged up closer behind her and gave her a shove. She tripped and fell forward into what looked like a ditch full of water. If she ever survived all this, she was going to have words with Al about his tendency to shove her into every puddle and mud pile on the planet.

As her head bobbed up out of the water, she saw Al on the lip of the ditch, his AR-15 pointed back toward Garson. He was returning fire, sparingly, while Garson seemed eager to use up every bit of ammo he was carrying. Maybe it was heavy or something.

Tanner barked during the first pause.

The guy was probably digging for and shoving in another clip.

"Let's go."

They took off running again. This time, she was on her own. Tanner might have kept up with her, but not Al.

"Keep going. Veer off to the right," Al called out to her. "I'll try to draw him away from you."

With Tanner at his side, Al ran toward his left, pausing to fire back behind him now and again. Soon, he was out of sight.

She ran as she had never run before, her feet slipping in the mud. Once or twice, she stumbled, fell onto her hands, then pushed herself back upright.

Nearly out of breath, she paused for just a second. Above the sound of sirens, now quite loud and close, she could hear footsteps splashing after her.

Damn. The guy hadn't taken Al's bait. He was following her. She took off at a run again. The sky was lightening, and she could see more clearly through the rain. But that meant this Garson could see her too. There was little cover. The ground was black where it wasn't covered in pools of water still dotted by the rain coming down. She spun and fired the Ruger toward the sound behind her.

She was answered by a spray of bullets. She ducked behind the black trunk of a tree just as the line of bullets got to her. She fired a couple of times from behind the tree before taking off in a flat-out run. Her lungs were burning, and her side began to hurt, but she pressed herself to run on and run faster.

Shots sent up sprays of water around her. She ducked and veered until she was behind a stand of black sticks that used to be trees or shrubs of some sort—not cedar or they would have burned to the ground like candles.

Fergie had been saving her shots. She knew she was down to the final one.

Shots sprayed into the spot where she'd just been. She ran up a small slope, tripped as she crested the hill, and fell into a muddy creek flowing swiftly enough to have the white crests of waves in rapids as the water rushed down an arroyo toward lower ground.

Any other time, the water might have felt refreshing. But she struggled to stand in it then reached to its edge to scoop up mud and rub it all over her face again.

She crouched as low as she could get, only her face and gun out of the cool water that poured across the rest of her.

AL HELD TANNER'S LEASH and moved as quickly as he dared across shiny, wet ground that seemed more slippery with every step.

The rain had become a steady white noise around him, no longer coming down hard enough to knock someone down. But it was relentless. The hard soil, baked by weeks of drought, wasn't helping, making the ground beneath him like a bathtub overflowing.

He paused, listening. Tanner tilted his head and seemed to be listening too.

Al should have heard loud footsteps sloshing along after him. He heard nothing. As far around him as he could see through the rain, he saw nothing.

"This isn't good," he whispered to Tanner. "That guy was supposed to have followed me."

He heard shooting break out in the distance, in the direction Fergie had gone.

There was nothing for it but to go back. He realized what Fergie had become to him. He could have stood losing himself to save the others, and even Tanner, but not Fergie.

He started to run, not sure what he'd find, but he had to go back. Tanner ran along beside him, sometimes surging ahead.

Silly scenarios ran through Al's head as panic set in. He couldn't picture life now without Fergie. Of course, he'd never told her that.

He slipped and fell onto his side. Tanner came back to see if he was okay. He was, but he was angry with himself.

"Come on, old man," he urged himself as he struggled to get back to his feet. "You can do this. You have to do this."

Al looked around as he ran, slipping and sliding half the time, only once falling to his knees. He kept going until he was pretty sure he was back to where he and Fergie had split up.

"Find her," he bent to whisper in Tanner's ear. "Find Fergie."

Tanner cast about, his nose low to the ground. Rain and wet weather are supposed to enhance the scents dogs can follow. But this torrent might have moved the trail, sweeping the odor of Fergie's steps away from the spot.

At last, Tanner got a whiff of something. His head rose up, and he took off at a full run. Keeping up took everything Al had.

"Be okay," he muttered to himself. "Please be okay."

GARSON KNEW HE WAS almost up to her. This was starting to feel like a fool's game. He could hear the sirens start to turn off as what he figured were cruisers pulled into the lot, with men probably scrambling out. But he was almost to the woman running. Even with one game leg, he figured he could take care of business and still slip away, getting clear in time.

All he could think of was that she was a witness, that she needed killing. His lungs were pounding and burning, but he forced himself to run more quickly.

He crested the slight hill and stopped. He couldn't see her anywhere. He heard a sound.

"Psst."

That was no snake. He looked down. It was the woman, with the barrel of a revolver pointed right at him. The last thing he saw, and would ever see, was the flame of a bullet being fired out the end of a .357 Magnum with a muzzle velocity of over 1,500 feet per second.

FERGIE STOOD UP AND waded out of the running water. She stood there, rubbing at the drying mud and at the tears starting down both cheeks, trying to wash the mud away.

Above the sound of the steady rain, she could hear what sounded like the sheriff's department SWAT team swarming in.

Someone grabbed her tightly and was holding her, gripping her in a hug. She rubbed at her eyes. "Is that you, Al?"

"Yeah. It's me. It'll always be me."

Chapter Thirty-Four

The relentless rain slowed gradually to a persistent drizzle.

Men shouted, and beams of light speared the sparkling sky and lit up stretches of blackened earth as the SWAT team swarmed closer.

Al and Fergie stood in the rain, each holding up a badge. Al was holding Tanner's leash with his other hand. The first men of the tactical squad found them and went through the usual shouting hysteria of finding two armed ratty-looking individuals who claimed to be cops, or former cops.

They stood in the rain for another five or six minutes. Al held Fergie's hand, and between them, Tanner pressed close against a leg of each of them.

Al was thinking, *It's hard to think "cozy little family" when you're standing here wet through to the skin.* So he said nothing. Even Tanner seemed to crave getting indoors, getting dried off, sitting by a fireplace. Maybe Al was reading that into the dog's frequent glances up at him.

At last the team's squad leader came up to them.

Al felt a pleasant ripple of surprise when the leader tugged off the mask tactical-team members wear, and there was Thelma Louise Simmons.

"Well, bless my heart," Fergie said. "I see Clayton is growing with the times and has promoted a worthy person up to a leadership spot."

"Stand down," Thelma Louise told the deputies holding Al and Fergie at gunpoint. "Some of you know Al, and I know Fergie. We liaised on a few projects in the past, though I was young and up-and-coming while she was... easing toward retirement, which she still apparently hasn't achieved all the way."

Thelma Louise didn't grin. Her job was too serious for that. But she did shake hands and indicated to the deputies that Al and Fergie could have their pistols back.

"Anyone still active and hostile here?" she asked.

"Not now," Al said.

To the nearest two deputies, she said, "Go with these two. They'll know where the bodies are, and knowing Al, there will be bodies."

Al and Fergie trudged through the pools of water and slick blackened muddy stretches of what had once been patches of tall prairie grass surrounding the trailer where scrub bushes and cacti had not taken over.

Huge stands of prickly-pear cactus, some of the last remaining green spots in the area, had been reduced to wrinkled, thornless black knots that looked more like wet burned licorice than any kind of plant.

The deputies they guided saw Fergie begin to shiver and felt enough pity to round up two blankets and a couple of long-handled flashlights.

SWAT team members had already found the body of Lee where Al had left him. Fergie showed them the way to Garson. When she told them how he'd died, they took the Ruger she'd used.

Al shrugged. When they asked for his Sig Sauer too, he just said, "No."

They looked at each other and didn't press the issue.

Tanner sniffed around then tugged at the leash Al held. He led them to where the FBI agent Jim Perkins lay, still cuffed wrists to ankles. The SWAT team members must have been running right past him.

He was half covered by water in a gentle arroyo while arching his back and stretching to keep his face and nose above the water that trickled steadily over him on its way down the slope.

He cussed steadily, sharing some language that would embarrass longshoremen as the deputies unlocked the cuffs and freed him.

"An agent in charge named Bradley says you're to call him first thing," one of the deputies told him. "He apparently wishes to have words with you."

Jim's mouth snapped shut at that. He started to dig in his pocket for his cell phone.

Al figured the agent perhaps knew of a procedural step or two he might have done differently. Such were the inscrutable ways of the FBI that Al doubted he and Fergie would be privy to much if any of that.

Just about tired enough to lie right down in the drizzle and mud, Al kept an eye on Fergie, who stumbled and slipped a couple of times but didn't fall. She had to be as tired and as emotionally spent as he felt.

Tanner pressed as tightly against Al's legs as he could. Al reached down to scratch Tanner's wet head.

Most of Thelma Louise's team had gathered near what was left of the trailer. Al could hear the blare of a fire engine coming this way, adding its noise to the ruckus. Most of the fire inside the trailer appeared to have died out in the rain. Al could see black scorch marks on the side of the fuel tank. They were all fortunate that it hadn't blown.

The ME's silver Volvo station wagon came waddling slowly along the soggy lane toward them. Al thought he could see Clive Barnes behind the wheel and his assistant Teddy beside him.

"Well, Al, what have you done this time?"

Al turned his head.

Victor Kahlon came splashing his way through puddles toward them. Though he was in the street clothes allowed to sheriff's department detectives, he wore the usual department cowboy hat with a clear plastic cover over that.

"Victor." Al held out a hand. "Late to the party, as usual. What brings you out here at this hour?"

"Apparently, it's standard procedure these days to wake up poor Victor every time another colorful Al Quinn moment takes place."

"Not my doing," Al said. "I was just swept along in this direction in my search for the dreaded chupacabra."

"One of the deputies found it, by the way, and Marvin is on his way here to represent the animal-control aspect here."

"Was it dead?" Al asked.

"Very."

"You'd better give Maury and Bonnie a ring to bring the Civic around," Al said to Fergie. "They'll need to explain one or two things from their end."

She stepped off a few strides and dug out her phone.

Al glanced up at the still-dark sky.

"If you're looking for the usual media copters, there's not enough visibility, and the attention is elsewhere. Clayton has deputies pulling overtime to keep back what few media have arrived out here until we can turn all this over to the feds."

"Still, since this is supposed to be so high profile, I would have expected some of them to be pushing harder," Al said. "I'm surprised they're not."

"That's because they're meeting outside the FBI offices even as we speak to get the initial briefing on how the FBI spearheaded the attempted capture and regrettable demise of the two who killed Senator Bentley."

Al shrugged. Fergie put away her phone and came over to him. He put an arm around her shoulders.

"Does that bother you, Al?" Victor asked. "Them getting the credit."

"I only worry about the important things, and that's not one of them."

"I've got to go tell Clive to hold off." Victor nodded toward Clive's Volvo. "The shooters' bodies are soon going to be on the way to the

FBI's ME in Austin. The rest of anything out here they'll be going over in their usual way. All we have to do is clear off and be out of their way."

"Who gets the chupacabra?"

"I understand Bradley said we could have it." Victor chuckled.

"Always nice to get something." Al's blanket had slipped down off his shoulder earlier while holding Tanner's leash when the dog had led them to the handcuffed Bureau agent.

Victor leaned closer. "Are you bleeding, Al? I thought that was someone else's blood on you."

"Just a little. No big deal."

"Stay right here. I'll get someone headed this way to take a look. We've already got an EMS wagon on the way. One of the Bureau guys needs a look as well."

Victor spun and took off in a careful jog that threw up splashes until he was out of sight.

Chapter Thirty-Five

The sun was barely coming up. The clouds had parted, and the sun was breaking through on the eastern horizon. Al couldn't quite hear the "Hallelujah Chorus" kicking in, but he could imagine it. What he could hear was water dripping off the singed limbs of the remaining trees. Most of the grass around the trailer was burned low to the blackened ground.

Al sat on the back end of an EMS truck while the young male EMS medic started to cut away part of his shirt then just took it all the way off him. Whenever he had to partially disrobe in public, Al was always glad for those hours he spent at the gym.

"You're pretty fit for someone of your years," the medic said.

"Are you coming on to me?" Al asked.

The medic glanced toward Fergie.

"He's just messing with you," Fergie said. "He thinks that sort of thing is clever."

The medic gave an uncertain grin and swabbed away at the groove a bullet had made across the fleshy part of Al's shoulder. "We should have you patched up and ready to go in no time," the techie said. "You're sure lucky."

"Yeah, that's Al. He's sure one lucky sort of guy." Clayton stood looking at his trailer.

FBI Special Agent E. J. Scholling lay stretched out on the gurney inside the EMS vehicle. His partner, Jim Perkins, sat inside the vehicle too and watched as the techie there redressed the wound on E. J.'s arm. "The shot pellets will have to come out of your face when we get to the hospital, and you're going to need rabies shots too," the medic said.

"The sheriff's department animal-control guy says that thing was almost certainly rabid, or it wouldn't have acted like that."

"And it wasn't any darn chupacabra either," Clayton said, loud enough for them to hear. "Marvin says this was a coyote with mange, and yeah, it was almost certainly rabid. He'll know more after tests, but I'd go ahead with the shots, painful though they are. Hell, get as many as you want of them."

"I'll take the SUV and meet you at the hospital." Jim patted his partner on the arm. He stepped around where Al sat and hopped out of the back of the EMS vehicle.

He looked over at where the ME's men were taking two body bags to another waiting vehicle. "Yep." Jim nodded. "We always get our men. Best record in the Bureau."

Clayton turned away to share an eye roll with Al.

Jim started off toward the SUV he'd brought around close after Thelma Louise's SWAT team had given the all clear. He had recovered a little strut to his stride, especially amazing for someone in rumpled clothes who not long before had been found handcuffed hands to feet in a ditch of water.

The techie finished the taping on Al's shoulder. "That should do it. None of your folks had anything to do with that rabid animal, did you?"

"Not the way he did." Al nodded toward E. J. on the gurney.

When Al stood, the techie closed the back of the vehicle and went around to the driver's seat. He hopped in and started it up. The ambulance was soon rolling out of sight.

"Are rabies shots still as painful as they used to be?" Fergie asked.

"Unfortunately, no," Al said. "And they haven't shot them in the stomach since the 1980s. Nor are there thirty shots, only four or so to the deltoid muscle of the upper arm."

"Too bad." Fergie stood close by, holding Tanner's leash. She glanced around, even into the sky around them. A lone news-network copter circled the area, but none of the media vans had been allowed through. "Still not much media. That's amazing. Wasn't this a pretty high-profile mess?"

"Indeed it was and still is. The media are being dealt with elsewhere. That's the way I wanted it. I let it happen that way," Clayton said. "You see, I'm more than a bit like Al here. I like my privacy."

"Al does like that," Fergie said.

Clayton nodded. "I spoke with Bryan C. Richards, the state's top agent in charge over in Houston. He agreed to have Benjamin Omar Bradley, the Austin office's special agent in charge, deal with the media. Those two agents you met were out of Bradley's office. Richards says they're a little rough around the edges, but they seem to get the job done. You can trust me that Richards isn't nearly as bamboozled as the media and the public. A protocol was in place where any of Bradley's teams that spotted the shooters were to let him know immediately. That call never happened." Clayton let out a harsh breath. "That wouldn't sail with me."

"I doubt it would," Al said, trying to get his shirt back on right.

Fergie saw him struggling and stepped in closer to help. She handed Tanner's leash to Maury. He stood beside the Honda Civic they'd pulled up close. Bonnie was sitting inside on the back seat. Because of the blanket she'd borrowed from the EMS crew and had thrown over her chest, Al guessed she was breastfeeding the baby.

Clayton stared at what was left of his trailer getaway.

Al hoped no mementos or valuable fishing gear or anything was in there. "I'm sorry as hell about your trailer," he told Clayton.

Clayton shrugged. "The missus has been after me to upgrade the trailer. I'm way over-insured on it, so it looks like she got her wish."

He took in the blackened ground in all directions. "The scrub was getting out of hand around here too. I just spoke with a land-clearing crew that said they could do the job for fifteen hundred bucks. So that's money saved and left in the bank."

The last of the fire trucks fired up and pulled out. The SWAT team had gone back to their base some time ago.

"I'd better be going too," Clayton said. "I have about a zillion reports to get done after this little kerfuffle. And I'd like to get clear of here before those fed folks are clomping all over the place."

"What about us?" Fergie said. "Al and I had to do some things to get Bonnie and Maury out safely. I mean, there were bodies."

Clayton looked at Al. "You tell her."

"It's cleaner this way. The FBI had a lot of people involved in this, and the guys we met were only a couple of them. Other teams and tactical squads were poised to sweep in since this was such a high-profile case. Their team fed them info requested, like where Bonnie was located once Maury called her. But as the public has already begun to hear, the two guys who were on the scene first handled the shooters on their own."

"They did?" Maury asked.

"Yep," Clayton said, "and if anything needs to be done about their basic grasp of procedures, it can be done with a reboot quietly by Bradley within the big Bureau machine."

"They need a boot, all right," Fergie huffed.

"Think of it this way," Clayton said. "You don't get hours of tedious explanation and cross-examination. No need for lengthy reports, except to me. You get to go home."

"You've always been so up front and transparent. Doesn't this rankle?" Fergie asked.

Clayton's mouth twisted to one side for a second. "All the way to my back teeth. But the public wants closure on the death of a senator—"

"And abuser of women," Fergie said.

"That too. So, ready to scoot on home?"

Fergie pursed her lips and looked at Al. "I think I can live with that. You?"

"I practically have my slippers on already."

Bonnie set aside the blanket and straightened her blouse as she stepped out of the back of the Civic.

"So there never was a chupacabra?" she asked.

"We can't say that," Clayton said. "We can just say *this* wasn't one. My animal-control people will have a vet do an autopsy to confirm if it was rabid. If any of the media ever does get next to any of you, which I'm hoping never has reason to happen, please don't say the word *chupacabra*. Got it?"

Al and the others nodded.

"Well, I'll see you in the funny papers." Clayton pulled his hat down tighter and started for his cruiser. He got in, started it, and was soon fading out of sight along a lane as blackened as the burned grass on either side of it.

Chapter Thirty-Six

Fergie drove, and Al got to look out his window at a wasteland pretty bleak in spots as they followed Clayton's cruiser along a bumpy path that brought them out behind the rows of sheriff's department cruisers and media vans, which were soon behind them.

"I feel bad about losing the stuff of ours in the trailer," Maury said, looking back through the rear window.

"Clayton lost plenty too," Fergie said.

"Wasn't like he had much personal stuff in there," Bonnie said, "like a collection of Hummel figurines or anything."

"Still and all, it'll cost him to replace quite a bit of what was inside," Al said.

"Speaking of replacing, we need to stop for diapers," Bonnie said.

"I wasn't going to say anything," Maury said, "but please do."

Fergie obliged a few miles later by pulling into a Circle K convenience store. Although a few parking spaces were open at the front of the store, she parked over behind the air pump, where they could get out and stretch their legs for a moment.

Maury shot off inside the place, coming back in moments with a package of diapers, which he handed off like a football to Bonnie as she headed for the restroom.

Al was hard pressed to remember if he had ever imagined Maury as a concerned parent. *Nope.* The thought had never in the years past crossed his mind.

By the time Bonnie came back outside carrying Little Al, already asleep on her shoulder after his change, the others were standing around with Styrofoam cups of coffee. She laid the baby down on the back seat but left the door open. Maury held out a coffee for her.

Al held a small package of mini donuts heavily dusted with sugar.

Normally, Fergie might have curled a lip at that, but she must have figured Al had burned enough calories to deserve a break.

Al broke off half his donut and gave it to Tanner, who gulped it down. He handed the rest of the package to Bonnie.

She sat down on the edge of the seat beside Little Al, glanced his way to confirm he was sleeping, then took a sip of coffee and a bite of donut.

Maury leaned in over her shoulder to look at the baby. "Quite a day."

"It's a shame we never got that money back for the hospital fund," Bonnie said with a mustache of white sugar on her upper lip.

Al grinned. "Who said we didn't?"

"You did? But when?" Maury asked.

"Did you know that a million dollars in one hundreds weighs twenty-two pounds?"

"And?"

"That means your two hundred and seventy thousand weighs about six pounds." Al went to the back of the Civic and reached inside to pop open the trunk. He went around to it and took out the small canvas bag, which was much lighter without any weapons inside. "Take a look inside." He put it down on Bonnie's lap.

Maury zipped it open. He and Bonnie both bent to peer inside.

"I can't believe it," Bonnie said.

"Why didn't you say anything at the time?" Maury asked. "You must have taken it from Cynthia's Town & Country way before that attorney general's guy took her vehicle away."

"Welcome to the way Al's chess-playing head works," Fergie said. "Always one step ahead and sharing very little until he needs to."

"It was best to stay focused on getting back to the trailer and making sure Bonnie and the baby were okay," Al said, frowning down at the state of his clothes, especially the shirt.

"It's all one step at a time with him," Fergie said. "I don't mind, as long as they're the right steps."

Al stayed focused on his torn shirt and on the gauze showing through the tear. He tugged at the cloth until the white tape barely showed.

"Let me ask you just one thing," Fergie said.

"Is it about Sidney Draper?"

"Of course it is." Fergie brushed his hand away from his shirt and lifted his chin so that he had to look into her eyes. "Did you reach out to him to let him know, or was yours just a remarkable hunch?"

"Hunch."

"What the heck are you guys talking about?" Maury asked.

"You have to remember, Maury, that I'm a detective too," Fergie said. "I've been sifting through a number of seemingly surprising moments that didn't seem to surprise Al at all as he worked in his usual mysterious way his wonders to perform."

"Okay, you've lost me now too," Bonnie said.

"Al has us stow our weapons in the trunk. He drives Cynthia's vehicle. He's the least surprised of us when Draper and a bunch of troopers are poised outside Luther's ranch."

"Yeah, what about that, Al?" Bonnie asked.

Al sighed. "Fergie and I ran into Draper in the Houston area. I mentioned Cynthia's name, and his eyes didn't light up or anything. He was like a stone. That was his tell, the way someone from the AG's office would look eager, by being the opposite of eager."

"What?" Maury asked.

"I get it," Fergie said. "Even *you* might have trouble at a poker table with one of those guys, Maury."

Al nodded. "He's zooming all over the state, looking under the carpet for frauds and scams. Maury's smack dab in the middle of a snake's nest of such people. I figured Draper would land there soon, especially after Luther explained why he had thugs on hand, because he'd stung some rich old cattle gal with political connections. All the chatter about cartels was the usual scamster hooey. If she didn't send some rodeo-tough cowhands after him to rough him up, she'd probably go to the AG's office. So I figured Draper would be close. When the alarm went off in there while we had most of the key players locked in a room where they couldn't set it off, I figured Draper had someone inside, a so-called student or teacher, who had a better than fair idea of what was going on with us."

"Yet no one did anything to help us," Maury said.

"We were playing out roles that added to the hard evidence Draper needed to act. Whether we made it out or not, he had enough on Luther to act at last. He probably had a better hunch about how Cynthia banked than we did, which is why I took out the amount you guys had lost before we left the spot where we'd hid the Civic. If he hadn't stopped us on the road, I'd have had to get Cynthia's vehicle to him some other way."

Al's eyes swept the others but settled on Fergie. "So, yeah, I *was* surprised when Draper and those troopers were poised right outside that ranch, but not as surprised as you. His being there was a logical contingency, one I had to anticipate. Not telling you three about having tucked away the cancer-fund money was to prevent anyone from letting Draper know about that. What you didn't know, you couldn't accidentally share."

"And there," Fergie said, "is the convoluted sort of thinking that got us to where we are today, with the missing money back, sans government red tape, and us quietly in the background while Draper rakes in credit for busting Cynthia, Luther, and who knows how many other scammers out at that ranch. Al was willing to traipse all over the state, spend his own money, and even get shot in the bargain, all for no reward or credit. You see, that's the thing Clayton was hinting about Al. All he wants to do is, in the end, be left alone."

"I guess our presence must really be starting to bug him until he's cross-eyed," Bonnie said.

"Oh, I think we're wearing him down," Fergie said. "In a good way."

Al reached to rub Tanner's head. "Yeah, you're all welcome... and part of the family now." When he looked up, his eyes locked with Fergie's.

"What happens if the attorney general's office honors our claim for the amount one of these days?" Maury asked.

"I'd take it," Fergie said. "It'll be ill-gained money that woman chiseled out of somewhere. Add it to your total and consider it the best fundraiser ever. Are your ethical qualms okay with that, Al?"

"I guess so," he said. "If no one else who got ripped off doesn't put in a claim for it, and if it's for the cancer charity and not going into our pockets, I can't squawk."

"So there you have it," Fergie said. "All this, including Al getting wounded, wasn't for nothing. It may well mean a lot for cancer research, just the way you wanted, Bonnie."

"If that does happen," Bonnie said, "we're going to have to at the very least consider that Cynthia, Cat, or whatever the hell her name is is a really fine rainmaker indeed."

"Well, I'm glad that's settled," Maury said, "and that we'll still have our jobs."

"I'm just looking forward to everything getting back to normal," Al said, "and it being so quiet we have a chance to be bored."

Bonnie said to Fergie, "I do believe you may yet domesticate the animal that is Al."

Fergie just grinned and said nothing. She didn't need to.

About the Author

Russ Hall is author of fifteen published fiction books, most in hardback and subsequently published in mass market paperback by Harlequin's Worldwide Mystery imprint and Leisure Books. He has also co-authored numerous non-fiction books, most recently *Do You Matter: How Great Design Will Make People Love Your Company* (Financial Times Press, 2009) with Richard Brunner, former head of design at Apple, *Now You're Thinking* (Financial Times Press, 2011), and *Identity* (Financial Times Press, 2012) with Stedman Graham, Oprah's companion.

His graduate degree is in creative writing. He has been a nonfiction editor for major publishing companies, ranging from HarperCollins (then Harper & Row), Simon & Schuster, to Pearson. He has lived in Columbus, OH, New Haven, CT, Boca Raton, FL, Chapel Hill, NC, and New York City. Moving to the Austin area from New York City in 1983.

He is a long-time member of the Mystery Writers of America, Western Writers of America, and Sisters in Crime. He is a frequent judge for writing organizations.

In 2011, he was awarded the Sage Award, by The Barbara Burnett Smith Mentoring Authors Foundation—a Texas award for the mentoring author who demonstrates an outstanding spirit of service in mentoring, sharing and leading others in the mystery writing community. In 1996, he won the Nancy Pickard Mystery Fiction Award for short fiction.

Read more at www.russhall.com.

About the Publisher

Dear Reader,

We hope you enjoyed this book. Please consider leaving a review on your favorite book site.

Visit https://RedAdeptPublishing.com to see our entire catalogue.

Don't forget to subscribe to our monthly newsletter to be notified of future releases and special sales.

www.ingramcontent.com/pod-product-compliance
Lightning Source LLC
Chambersburg PA
CBHW050519190726
48284CB00003B/870